RING OF SMOKE

RING OF SMOKE

By Felix Flores, Jr.

Published by
MIDNIGHT EXPRESS BOOKS

RING OF SMOKE

Published by
MIDNIGHT EXPRESS BOOKS
POBox 69
Berryville AR 72616
(870) 210-3772
MEBooks1@yahoo.com

RING OF SMOKE

By Felix Flores, Jr.

ACKNOWLEDGEMENTS

I wish to thank some of my fellow inmates for taking time to put up with me while I wrote *RING OF SMOKE,* J. D. Freeman, Juan Jose Jasso, and Ronald "Butch" Holman. You each helped with your feedback.

I also like to dedicate this book to my son Gabriel and my beloved Mother, who I forever will keep in my prayers.

All my loved ones I've lost as I've sat here in prison may you all rest in peace and God bless you. Also to the guards who thought this book was worthy of publishing.

My warmest "Thank You's" go out to "M.E.B." Midnight Express Books for helping inmates such as myself.

No matter where you are, never give up on your hopes and dreams. Everything is possible with faith in your heart.

I hope you like this book and more to come.

Felix Flores, Jr.

August 2013

CHAPTER 1

Through the middle of worn out wooden slabs of an old abandoned stable, streaks of light shot into the cold late night darkness. As the wind blew its force upon the weakened stable, sounds of distant wolves howling could be heard inside. But keeping a fire burning would be a must, for a human body could easily freeze in the middle of the night...Not knowing how long the storm would take to ease up enough to at least have a chance, to make it into the nearest town was really not much of a concern to the rugged cowboy. For this by far not being Bill Truette's first rodeo with blizzards would tell, yet only he would be the keeper in knowing the struggles life had brought his way.

Knowing that the sounds of wolves in the distance could be, and most likely was, a band of Indians. The thought of Indians would bring chills to anyone's body, but being brave took a certain type of man to outwit and live to tell about it or even care to speak of it. At least the cold windy storm would hold off an attack for the moment. For food and rest promise a new beginning as the dawn's light would once again appear.

Staring into the fire, Truette could still see his family tied down to the ground with little cuts all over their bodies as wooden spikes had been used to hold them down. Being left to be eaten by ants as each had been doused with honey. Something Indians had mastered when punishing an enemy, yet the clues told another story because Indians never put horseshoes on their horses or even wore cowboy boots as the ground held the true story of what had happened.

The trails had become unable to follow because of the blizzard. Only one clue was left to know which way the four riders had gone. Northbound would take them to the mountains where the gold rush was at hand.

Dozing off into a deep sleep was what Truette had needed. For he'd not slept in three days and had only eaten once because of the rage within his soul. Having to find all his loved ones dead except his wife Amy, was enough to want to kill, yet having to bury them only made his hate a way of life, for each one who was involved.

With the knowledge that there had only been four riders because of the clues on the ground, who had done what they pleased, didn't make much sense, but the blame was only his to bear for leaving them alone. Riding off into the distance in search of a baby calf which may have already become the dinner of wolves or a mountain lion. It would be a miracle if found. But the love of his horses and cattle made it simple. He had to go in search for the small calf. Far away into a small pit in a grassy field, the calf would not have made it out alone. Until Truette had found it crying for its mother.

Throwing the calf across the saddle and returning it to the herd would ease the cowboy's mind and momentarily bring a sense of pride to his heart. Returning to the ranch, the silence in the air would speak to any man, and Truette knew something was wrong. What he'd found would linger in his mind forever.

A lifelong dream which had become true; a wife and children, along with a ranch filled with cattle and horses with the brand "PG" had been stripped away in a moment that left an anger instilled in the man. Now on the trail of four men who did it was also gone because of the blizzard as well as another night in his life.

On the trail of four enemies that Truette could not put a face on, or figure out why they'd done what they had. Also no telling how many enemies of the white man were behind, had made the odds even more dangerous. The cowboy could easily walk into a death trap if they would come to know a lone rider was behind them. Yet moving too slow would get him caught asleep because Indians could creep up on a rattlesnake if they wished. Yet stuck between two types of killers would also make Truette a killer himself, if life or death were his choices. As before in his life, men had died in trying him or even bring the cowboy to kill when his life was in danger.

Forgiveness was not an option for the cowboy. For when he caught up to the four riders. Death would be the only retribution for what they had done. Dreaming of his wife Amy and children had caused the cowboy to toss and turn as his eyes tightened up all the more as he slept. The crow's feet wrinkles on Truette's face showed the true hurt within his soul. Whispers of his wife Amy and his children echoed in the cowboy's mind and the dream seemed so real. Yet something had come to stop the cries of his family. It grew louder and louder, but whatever it was had caused the cowboy to sit straight up, gun in hand, ready to shoot the sound now coming from inside the stable, not from outside. Rolling quickly to one side and almost to the point of letting his gun go off, a small shape in the corner of the stable now stood looking at him. Standing bravely, the shape was making a stance for life, but somehow a smile came onto the cowboy's face as the fear subsided. Calling out to a baby wolf to come to him, it growled as if to show its bravery, yet playful as it wagged its tail and crept over to the cowboy. Holding the baby wolf close to him for warmth and an assurance of not being harmful, Truette spoke to it asking if its mother or father would be close by. The baby wolf had become the watchdog to sound an alarm if someone or something were to approach. All the cowboy had to offer to feed his new friend was some dry beef jerky along with water from his canteen.

Truette didn't know that a friend for life had just been made. Somehow the baby wolf had gone astray from its pack and ended up at the stable. As the cowboy sat looking at the baby wolf eat and drink, he could feel it had been a while since the little fellow had a meal. Looking at the baby wolf while rolling a cigarette, the cowboy noticed that the baby wolf never took its eyes off him. As the cowboy lit up the cigarette, the baby wolf stopped to see the smoke in the air, tilting its head from side to side as he blew rings of smoke into the air. Smiling at his new friend, the cowboy told the baby wolf that his name was Truette and that its name would be "Ring of Smoke". The baby wolf howl as he blew yet another ring of smoke into the air. The cowboy stood up and walked over to where his horse was within the stable. He told him that the baby wolf would be a new member of their family.

Truette was thinking that this baby wolf could be or come in handy as his sixth sense, but a trust would have to be created and a special bond would as well have to be made. For now playing with his new friend would keep the cowboy's mind at ease. Adding a few more boards of wood to the fire, from a broken down ladder that layed on top of a wagon wheel would keep the stable warm and provide light to see around. Rusted nails held an old pair of spurs with double-spike stars on each, which told the cowboy they had been used to break wild stallions some time ago... Maybe this stable was a stop to get supplies and rest earlier in time. Also a ranch was built, yet only a half a wall stood here and there which would not be enough to shelter anyone in any kind of bad weather. From the squeaks and groans coming from the stable, it would someday soon collapse to the ground.

In another corner of the stable was a large iron kettle which had been used as a fire keeper for branding. The branding iron was hanging from hooks over the kettle. Holding it up to the light of the fire, Truette could still see the brand symbol in good shape "HD". Looking around the stable, the cowboy spotted a small door leading to a room of some kind. But this would have to wait until daylight so he could see better. Setting the double-spiked star spurs next to his saddle, along with the branding iron from the kettle, the cowboy decided to take them with him.

The unknown reason to carry his newly found treasures was puzzling. Maybe he was just a pack rat of odd things.

From the corner of his left eye, a small shape sped across the ground. Into a hole in the dirt as light from the fire had given enough light. He could tell this was no ordinary rodent, but a kangaroo rat, a desert dweller that was able to survive on little water. This small rodent got all the moisture it needed from dry seeds. Once in a while, a scorpion would appear, but slowly crawl back under anything waiting on its next meal.

Devil's Den Desert, when not hit by cold blizzards, hardly got any snow as it slices through North Clayton and up into Galloping Stones. Often times, desert dwellers such as kangaroo rats, coyotes, roadrunners, bobcats, jack rabbits, bighorn sheep, javelins, feral hogs, quail, white-tailed deer, mule deer, turkeys and pheasants depended on getting water from cactus spines, leaves or flowers. Some got juices from other animals they ate. But the ones to keep an eye out for were diamondback rattlesnakes. One bite could turn anyone's life around or even cause death.

As the dawn's light began to come into the stable, the cowboy's eyes now focused on the little baby wolf that stood at the entrance of the doorway. Opening the door was now a must, for the baby wolf seemed to be telling the cowboy something was inside. Knocking off the doorknob with the branding iron, the door slowly creaked open and the baby wolf ran inside straight atop a wooden box. The baby wolf howled a low spooky howl inside that sent chills through Truette's body and told the cowboy it was a must to open the box.

Slowly dragging the box out of the room into the middle of the stable, he had to use the old branding iron to open it. It had been nailed shut for so many years, or so it seemed. The box appeared to be just one solid piece of wood.

Once opened, the box contained a cloth which held oily materials and when it was unrolled; it had been used to cover a holster with the gun still intact. Pulling the gun out of the holster was like pulling a hot knife out of butter, smoothly slipping out without once feeling like it had been put away for so long. Whoever had been the owner of the gun took good care of it, yet for some strange reason, the gun had been stored away. Rolling his bed roll up Truette was puzzled at the letters on the spurs, branding iron, and now on the handles of the gun. Who could "HD" be and where could this person be? Only made the cowboy wonder more, but taking them all seemed like the right thing to do and he'd worry about it later. Stuck for another endless night of dreams he wished would not happen, only turned into more nightmares as the baby wolf's howls saved him from going off into more of them. The dawn's next day's light told the cowboy the storm was over.

Putting out the fire, the cowboy now had to leave because it wouldn't be too wise to stay in one place too long. The storm had eased enough to ride out into Devil's Din Desert edges which only promised death. No clues or trails to follow, only common sense told the cowboy which way to go and as before it would be into the mountains. Stories once told that another world would always be on the other side of a mountain, and to escape the world the four riders had just been in was exactly what they had hoped for.

Riding away from the stable, Truette wondered why the branding iron, spurs, holsters with gun had been left, all with the same letters on each seemed quite odd. Yet upon leaving the stable, he'd also noticed the letters once again. On the side of the stable doors branded "HD" as he closed them and rode away. Growling the baby wolf looked up ahead, but the cowboy knew it was because of the ride on the horse's saddle, which "Ring of Smoke" had never experienced. In a few miles the cowboy would let him down to run or walk behind the horse. Just maybe he'd wait until Crystal Pit Canyon was in sight, at the outskirts of Devil's Den Desert. The canyon had gotten its name because of the many predators and preys eyes at night which were said to sparkle at a glance of moonlight. A place no man should fall asleep at night...at least not alone.

Felix Flores, Jr.

CHAPTER 2

Days had passed since the old stable had provided shelter, but most worries had left because no storms seemed to be at hand. Camp fires at night would easily give away one's spot in any area and at midday they only made smoke which would tell on you as well. But the chances had to be taken, because a cowboy was not a cowboy if he didn't drink hot black coffee and smoke tobacco. Being fast with a gun wasn't in the cowboy's talents, but hitting a target was no trouble. A six shooter was to always be with a man at all times out in the wild, as well as in town. In fact, when a boy was born, a baby bottle seemed to become a gun as he became a man.

The rifle was a means to use when hunting and the hunt was on, but not for food. Only to hunt down the four riders as death would be the only way to please his mind. To make them suffer never crossed his mind. Only Indians knew how to make a white man suffer slowly before death. And somewhere or somehow the four riders had learned to tie down someone to the ground with small cuts all over the bodies and pour honey or sugar on them so ants would leave nothing unless someone would find them, as the cowboy had done. His wife Amy was still alive but would slowly die because of blood lost from the ant bites. But his decision to fire a bullet into her heart would never be erased from his mind.

The children, one small girl, Patty Ann and two small boys, Bob and Jerry, were dead because of too much blood lost from the ant bites.

Before the cowboy had to shoot his own wife, he had told her in her ear, "I love you." Only one word was spoken by Amy before he had shot her which was "Infantry" or was it "Infinity?"

The words rang in Bill Truette's mind, but which word had it been? Could his wife Amy been giving him a clue? Were they foot soldiers or was she simply saying that her love was forever?

Finding the four riders was a must, killing them would be a pleasure. But why were the Indians after him or were they as well after the four riders? Time would tell and needing to know was also a must for the cowboy's mind wasn't functioning as it should have been. Walking next to his horse gave a moment of silence to battle thoughts of anger, which arose from time to time as in between the emotional effects would capture Truette's need to rush into his will to lust for death. A death each one of the four rides was promised if caught.

Late in the afternoon, it would cool off enough to find some shade and within the periods of rest, a cup of coffee and a bite to eat would bring voices in the wind. The voices of his wife Amy and children hid behind each breeze of wind. But it seemed that Ring of Smoke, the baby wolf, was the key to keeping Truette's mind stable. Wondering off into thoughts of loneliness, the baby wolf would howl into the sky, bringing the cowboy back to real life. As if the baby wolf had been sent into the cowboy's life to guide and yet so small it seemed as if it were the protector at the moment.

Realizing it was getting late in the afternoon a place to camp out for the night was to be found where shelter from the wind and maybe gunfire, if it ever came to that. Also a place where his horse could stand or lay down from the cold wind at nights.

While the sky began to form its brilliant colors of reddish purple and dark blue mixtures, a light dim orange at the bottom once again sent the cowboy's mind back to the night he'd found his loved ones at the ranch dead, except his wife Amy, who he had to shoot, brought a pain into his heart and his eyes began to sparkle as the tears made their way to the surface of his eyes.

Again the baby wolf's howls awoke the cowboy from another world that trapped his thoughts from the real one. As Truette glanced at the baby wolf with a smile, his horse reared up and pulling away from the cowboy, it showed a sign of fear nearby.

But what kind of fear only the horse and baby wolf could tell. Looking around the cowboy took a few more steps and heard the sound of rattlesnakes, but it was too late to catch himself as he'd stepped into a den of death and the pain that followed from the fangs which dug deep into his leg again and again. The only thing the cowboy could do was pull out as fast as he could and try to get to his scared off horse. This only caused him to stumble on a rock and hit his head on another rock that knocked him out cold.

Ring of Smoke's howls went out into the distance as the Indians that followed knew something was wrong. As if second nature took control, they came to the aid of the cowboy. For not only could the Indians master ways of pain given to an enemy, but also cure almost any illness and a snakebite was only a normal thing to do in the lives of their people.

Slices across the two fang holes a snake leaves after a bite was to be made, then sucking the cut to bring out as much poison as possible, was only to reduce the amount of venom that the snake had released. But that alone did not cure the person for it had to bleed out as much poison as possible. Then a special type of potion had to be made. Out in the wild cactus was used along with other plants the Indians knew how and where to gather. But the blow to the cowboy's head had caused him to go into a coma.

Only a medicine man knew how to cure or was believed to cure such an illness. The cowboy could have easily been scalped just as his family would have been many years ago. But the cowboy and his family were spared, and they remained in the watchful eyes of the Indian people as he now was. But why were these Indians following

Truette? Only they knew what the cowboy knew, or maybe he had found something they wanted. Whatever the reason, they didn't ever bother the cowboy or his family. But now it was very important to speak with the cowboy and in their hands laid the cowboy. Truette may not make it through the snake bites and if he did, the coma would take one day, maybe two, and even maybe forever to cure, if it was even possible to cure.

Indians always seemed to camp near a river. Not only because of water, but because it's been said that spirits flow over the running waters and medicine men from the tribes would speak to the spirits as they would dance around a fire calling for help from them. Wild weeds were smoked to ease their minds' flow of worries and bring a train of thoughts as well as a feeling of happiness to the body. Chanting and dancing was a way of life for the Indians. The people with no worries unless some other humans took or tried to take away from them. This tribe had been robbed of something that only a white man could go into the white man's face to get and it was a must to get back what had been taken from them. Whatever it had been only the Indians knew the reason. But somehow it had to do with the evil old man in town on the other side of the mountains which was Earl Hessenger.

Having the cowboy Truette in their hands now, punishment would not be required from the Indians, because once released, he could go do as he pleased or wished. So a means of helping the cowboy would have to take place in order for the cowboy to help them do what ever it was or wanted back from the enemies which took away something special.

Following Truette, the Indians already knew why he'd been after the four riders. As they had also seen the cowboy shoot his own wife in order to stop her suffering. They also witnessed him burying his family. They now knew he would kill if he had to.

Ring of Smokes' howls had saved the cowboy as the Indians arrived just in time. At least to help slow down the venom's poison and the flow of blood on top of the cowboy's head.

CHAPTER 3

Up ahead, the four greedy riders laughed at and with each other as each one wanted to become the leader. Refusing to take responsibility, of any wrong doings. Not caring for the wrongs behind their heels, only what they could get away with was their way of life.

In a nearby wooded area, the four riders had come across a stream. The cold running water would help to take away all the dirt and grime that weeks of not bathing had piled up on each one. Jumping carelessly into the water, none was smart enough to stay close to their guns and horses. Scattered clothes laid upon rocks in the edges of the stream as their guns were further away. Like the shadow of an eagle swooping down upon its prey, Indian warriors stood atop the edges of the stream where the four riders' clothes laid, looking into the eyes of the riders acting like fools do when drunk. But these four riders hadn't had a drink in days, yet it seemed as such.

Silence broke the noise as the four riders stared at the Indian warriors. If it hadn't been for the orders of the Chief to bring them back, arrows would be piercing each one by now. And if needed, an arrow may have been used to slow one down if they would try to run. Scared to death, each rider followed suit with hands in the air, climbing up to the top of the place where the Indians were pointing. It was a very clear point to move away from their rifles and guns.

Naked, each one was tied to one another in a row to walk them away. They were led onto a narrow trail leading back in the direction they had come from. They were being urged on with a shove now and then. Limping from the rocks and stickers, they were al lowed breaks once in a while. The first day's walk had ended in an open space with beautiful views of the night sky, shining moon light on the place that would be their camp to sleep for a bit.

Each rider would be tied down exactly as they done to Truette s family. But no punishment had been given so far and one of the Indians spoke to the others about how the Indians had no intentions of killing them because if they did, none of them would be alive at that point. Another rider mentioned that he wondered why or to where they were being taken, or if they would get a chance to escape if they could. Saddles had been left behind as well as the clothes, but their rifles and guns were brought along as their horses rode alone. No matter how long it took, the walk was a must and it was to give the other Indians enough time to get the cowboy back to the Indian camp.

After a week of walking, the four riders' feet were beginning to numb. If one failed to keep up with the others, he would be dragged slowly with a rope tied to one of the horses.

At times the Indians would stop for a rest to eat and give the riders food and water. But those moments of rest were very short.

Another day had passed as the four riders' skin was sunburned and blistered all across the front and back. Their eyes were swollen and their lips were badly cracked. Small portions of food and water were given, but it was meant to barely keep them alive.

In the distance, the four riders could see the cowboys' ranch where they had raped and tied to the ground the cowboy's wife and children. While standing there, one warrior took off into the direction of the ranch with the riders' four horses, releasing them into the meadow with the other horses with the "PG" brand on them. The ranch stood in the middle of an open meadow, beautiful to the human eye. Grassy fields full of flowers and trees that provided shade near a river of cold clear pure water. The view of the mountains was breathtaking and stretched for miles and miles. Each rider seeing the horses released into the meadow told them it would now be the reason of the things they had done to the woman and children at the ranch. Speaking to each other saying that they would have to try and get away because the Indian people were known to kill the white man for no reason. And to have a reason would only make it a slow torturous death none would enjoy. As the four riders began to panic, each one tried to place the blame on one another, showing the cowardice they all had started to show.

Arriving at the Indian camp, each of the four riders were tied to trees with buffalo hide strips of leather soaked in buzzard guts so when the strips dried, they would tighten up and if the skin tore open, an infection would start its toll of death. At the bottom of their feet, small cuts were made to keep them from running away if they did get the leather off their hands and arms. Once a day, another small meal was given to each, along with muddy water.

***

While lying in pain and numb from snake bites, the wound on his head from the fall had left a deep cut on the side of Bill Truette's head. Dreaming of the time many years ago where he'd worked as a ranch hand for an outfit that took good care of their help. They allowed the hands to keep their families with them.

His wife Amy, so beautiful, danced in his mind as she spoke of one day having a ranch of their own.

Then the letter or telegram had arrived from his sister that asked him to come and she needed help. The trip had taken a while because he couldn't leave his wife behind since she was due to have their child. But love held no boundaries and each moment with his wife was a dream come true. On the way to his sister's place, his wife had a beautiful little girl on the wagon trail riding through the roughest territory in the country. What he'd found at the ranch turned the dream into a nightmare, tossing and turning his head from side to side, he'd walked into the front door of the ranch and could see his sister's clothes torn off, her body looked like someone had taken turns raping her. She laid there with a knife still in her heart. Yards away on the floor, laid her husband with bullets in his chest.

Burying them in the graveyard that had been made on the side of the ranch, another grave had been there with the letters "PG" on a wooden cross. But the cowboy couldn't or wouldn't know who it could be. But all the livestock wore the letters as well as the entrance of the ranch's corral.

The dream had become a mist in his mind and the drama was too much to bear. Looking into the direction of the cowboy, the old Indian Chief could tell the cowboy was dreaming of someone or some past he'd loved. Speaking in Indian language, the Chief told the medicine man to blow wild smoke into the direction of the cowboy to ease his mind, thoughts and help him sleep. Peyote would do the trick once inhaled into his lungs.

As each day went by, at times the cowboy's eyes would open slightly and the vision of a young white skinned Indian warrior would appear passing by. The cowboy noticed the letters "PG" cruelly branded on his back as he passed by. Then the cowboy would doze off into another world of his own, as the echoes of his boss many years ago had told him to send word if he needed help...

Once in a while an old miner friend of the Indian Chief would bring the tribe bottles of whiskey as he'd stay and rest. In searching for gold, which he could never find a single pebble or even come across any dust which would say gold was around. On this visit, he was surprised to see what was in front of him.

Through the years the old miner had learned to speak the Indian language. Seeing the four riders tied to some trees and one on his back in some kind of pain. The old miner asked the Chief what had happened and he motioned to the young white warrior and said that he believed the cowboy in pain could be family and that the four who were tied up. Were the ones who killed the cowboy's wife and children. The Indian Chief called to the young warrior and told him to sit with them. He told him that the cowboy was or could be his family. As the old miner looked at the young warrior, he could see the letters "PG" plainly branded on his back and asked the Indian Chief what had happened. Of all the times the old miner had visited the camp, The Indian Chief never spoke of the young warrior due to the respect he had for the old miner and did not bring up the subject. But since it was concerning the cowboy and the young warrior, today would be a good time to tell the old miner. Listening to the Indian Chief say that when the young boy was left for death to claim his soul, the spirits spoke to him and told him to give the white young soul life again and bring him up as one of his own.

The old miner told the Indian Chief why had he waited so long to tell the young warrior and why not tell the cowboy when he'd first arrived at the PG ranch. The love of the young white boy had captured the old Indian Chief's heart and wanted to keep him forever. The cowboy never knew of the young warrior because the Chief had all the items the young child had be removed as well from the ranch. As the old evil man had done to the young white girl and had taken her away into the town over the mountains which belonged to the evil old man. This young white child was given a chance to live within the Indian people because the iron used to brand his back at the age of about three was enough to have killed him if left alone. But the Indian Chief had spared the young child's life and brought him up as his own son.

Tears falling down the young warrior's face made him fall to his knees and pound the ground with his fists...As he looked at the Indian Chief and told him it would be a must to go look for the evil old man. But the Chief told of the hundred men the evil old man had as hired hands to run the town. Also that the only way to get the girl back and kill the evil old man was to send a white speaking man into the town, but the one who had been chosen was out cold and was hurt at the time.

As days and nights took their place in the Indian camp, the young warrior would sit with the cowboy and wonder if in fact he was family, or just another cowboy who had taken over the ranch.

Felix Flores, Jr.

CHAPTER 4

Mr. and Mrs. Randalls had come to look for a new life in hopes to start a family and in the open meadows next to Devil's Din Desert they chose to build a ranch. As the years went by, it had taken time to build their dream and watch it unfold with happiness of being able to share their love with each other. One day while digging a trench to the ranch from a nearby river, they found pure gold rocks as they dug deeper.

Pure gold is what came out of the hole. So, Pure Gold was what they named the ranch. That's where PG branding iron had come from and all the stock wore. Mrs. Peggy Randalls wrote her brother Bill Truette in hopes to help him with gold they found but not mentioning anything about it in the telegram, only that he needed to come and help.

Needing supplies, Peggy's husband took a chance going into the evil old man's town, which had been the greatest mistake he ever made in his life. Taking a piece of gold was even more generous than anyone could ever have known, for the envy and greed took over any thoughts of buying the gold or letting Jake Randalls leave once again until the secret was told of where the gold had come from. On the floor of the hotel, which had gotten its name "Wagon Wheel" from the way the ceiling beams which held the first floor up resembled a real wagon wheel, laying face up, Jake Randalls was kicked until the evil old man,

Earl Hessenger, stepped into his view. The sting of the sharp spurs digging into his face cut across Jake's left cheek. As the evil old man spoke to his men to bring him outside to his horse as others brought more horses to ride out. Jake was to point the way out of town to where more gold would be found. Riding half beaten to death, Jake pointed the way as more gunmen joined in the ride. Leading back to the PG Ranch, Jake pointed at a spot close enough to allow his wife Peggy to see the riders digging which would also tell her to leave and take the children with her knowing Jake was giving her time to get away from the ranch. As she grabbed her young girl,

Sue, six years of age and her son Bobby, only three years old, she stopped next to the side of the ranch and dug a hole which was big enough to hold the potato sack full of rocks of pure gold. As she covered the hole back up and made a wooden cross with two pieces of wood from their picket fence, she then grabbed the pair of gloves off the ground next to the branding iron kettle. As she had done a hundred times before to brand the "PG" on her stock, she branded the wooden cross as she tossed the iron back into the kettle.

Trying to mount a horse was the only thing Peggy could remember as something hit her on the back of her head. Moments later, she awoke on the floor of her ranch. She came to only to find her husband being shot to death as bullets roared through his chest sending him crashing against the wall and onto the floor while his final reach for Peggy had taken only seconds to end and the body of her husband laid dead before her eyes. Sitting up and pulling her daughter next to her with her only son, she whispered to little Sue not to ever tell where the gold was. Little Sue in shock and tears told her mother she promised not to tell, as the gunmen tore her away from her mother, all the little three year old boy Bobby could do was run out the door as the men laughed at him saying that the only man in the house was running like a coward. The little girl Sue was thrown outside as Peggy's clothes were ripped off and the gunmen took turns on her, yet it would only be the beginning of her death as she was beaten and pierced with a knife through her heart all the way into the wooden planks of the floor. Laughing as the children ran away, the evil old man rode his horse along Sue's side. Picked her up from the back of her dress as he told her your mine from now on. As another rider motioned that the boy from the ranch was getting away, the evil old man rode next to the branding iron and told one of his gunmen to hand him a glove and the branding iron. He rode over to the man that had caught up to little Bobby and he branded the young boy's back with the PG branding iron. As he fell to the ground, passing out from the pain. Such a small child would be expected to die from.

The Indian Chief had gotten there too late to help anyone survive. Even if he had, his warriors would not have intervened because a white man's war was theirs, not the Indian people. But the evil old man from the town over the mountain needed death to touch his soul;

the sooner the better.

A few warriors were sent down to the ranch to find out if anyone was alive and the small boy was found passed out with a brand burned on his back. The child was burned real bad. But the Indian Chief ordered the warriors to remove all the items the boy had and bring him back to his camp. For he was to remember nothing of his past. The bodies of his mother and sister were to be left behind to dwell in the midst of the meadows.

The next morning was when Bill Truette (the cowboy) and his wife Amy had arrived at the ranch to find his sister and brother in law dead in their own home. Truette never knew they had any children, only that the letter was asking for help. No clues. No trails. Only the dead bodies which he would have to bury, but where? Looking for a place he came across the cross with PG and thought it was a grave of someone named PG. In time all Truette knew was that the ranch was named PG and all the livestock bore the brand as well. Thinking that PG must have been a special person to his sister Peggy and brother-in-law Jake. He would honor it and keep PG on everything from then on.

CHAPTER 5

As time went on Truette and Amy had two more children, Bob and Jerry, who could later come to help out on the ranch. All the dreams had come to an end as the dream was now a nightmare.

A few weeks had passed and The Cowboy would awaken from time to time as the Indian woman would wash him and laugh with him. Needing answers he noticed that the young white warrior would always be watching him. The healthier the Cowboy got the better he felt. The young white warrior would smile at the Cowboy as he noticed the PG letters on the back of the young warrior as he would walk away leaving the Cowboy wondering why were the letters PG branded on his back.

Singing, as the old miner rode his little donkey into the Indian camp, the Cowboy understood the words were English.

He stood up yelling at the old miner saying, Come over here, we need to speak to each other. Getting closer, the old miner told the Cowboy, Oh yeah, we sure do need to talk. Grab a hold of yourself; for this one is very touching. I have brought a lot of whiskey to pass around. As the old miner began to speak, his eyes rolled over and he fell to one side out cold, too drunk to speak any more as he had passed out.

At least the Cowboy had hoped to know what was going on. But for now as the old miner slept, all the young warriors came to the spot where the old miner was and sat as to take care of him. Early the next morning, the Cowboy stood over the old miner with food for him. As the old miner looked up at the Cowboy he asked him, where is my bottle of whiskey? The Cowboy looked into the eyes of the old miner to make sure he understood that he was not playing any more games. Telling Bill Truette the story from what the Indian Chief had said as the Chief stared into the Cowboy's eyes and pointed to the four riders. Letting him know they were the ones who had killed his family by making them suffer to death. The cowboy stood straight up with gun in hand heading to the area where the four riders were as the Indian Chief spoke in his native tongue, the young warriors stepped in the path of the cowboy. Then the old miner spoke to the cowboy that they would die a slow death in the hands of the young warrior for the way they had killed his family. He added that no more time could be wasted and the Cowboy had to ride into town to save the girl from the evil old man. The Cowboy spoke as the old miner translated back to the Indian Chief and asked why did they wait this long to tell him when he'd lived at the ranch all this time. The Chief had said that it was the love he had grown with the boy, but it would have to be told to the boy as well as Bill Truette.

The Chief wanted the cowboy to ride into town because no one knew who he was and he could find the girl who was now about sixteen or seventeen years of age. But he had to watch out for the Hessinger's gunmen who were always around him. The Chief also told the old miner to let the Cowboy know that Hessenger's men had killed his sister and brother-in-law at the PG Ranch, where the cowboy found them and buried them. The cowboy asked the old miner if the Chief knew who PG was. Could it be a man or a woman? As the old miner spoke to the Chief, he answered saying no one else had ever been seen, only the husband and wife with two young children. The Chief had no clue who PG could be...

Lowering his head, the old miner began to shed tears from his eyes as some memories floated to the top of his mind. Looking at the old miner, Truette asked him what the matter was. Pointing into the mountains, the old miner said that many years ago, he had a ranch which he'd built himself because of the view of the mountains and the beautiful meadows that surrounded them all and to leave would be like leaving a dream come true. Stopping for a moment to catch his breath, the old miner looked into the cowboy's eyes and said we need to leave it at that, for now.

Also that the only one who knew his past was the old Indian Chief but someday, maybe he would tell the cowboy about it.

The young warrior now knowing Truette was his uncle brought a joy to the young man's heart. Each day they sat with the baby wolf and the old miner spoke things that would need to be done to the ranch and things that the ranch might need. They started on a plan on how to go into town and try to bring the girl back home, if she even cared to.

As the four riders listened and pleaded for their lives, but death was the only reward for being the cowards they'd been when killing or leaving the cowboy's family to die. Alone the Cowboy would be the only one who could go into town and find the girl, but for now the four riders would have to be dealt with and a very slow death was the only way they would die. To Truette a bullet between the eyes would satisfy him, but now he would have to think of the ways the Indians had taught the young warrior how to give death a second thought and make an enemy suffer. Truette told the old miner to tell his nephew the young warrior that the punishment is handed down to the four riders as he'd wished because he'd have to leave now and not waste any more time. No telling what the young girl was going through if she was alive since it had been at least ten years when Hessenger who owned the town had taken her away. As the baby wolf made another howl into the late night sky, the Cowboy smiled as he called out his name "Ring of Smoke" to come to him. Once again the baby wolf had made the cowboy's day as they played together. But Ring of Smoke would have to stay behind with the Indian Chief and the young warrior.

CHAPTER 6

Arriving at the town, it had only taken a few yards into the streets as Truette had been watched from a very long distance before he was stopped. As the Hessenger's gunmen spoke to the Cowboy, one of them told him. (to look around you and think before you try anything stupid) and that each and every one of the hired gunmen were very quick and deadly with guns. Leading the Cowboy into the stable as with any stranger on orders of the evil old man Earl Hessenger, the Cowboy now stood surrounded by many gunmen, each watching his every move. Then one spoke again telling the Cowboy to walk towards the hotel very slowly. Entering the hotel, Hessenger sat looking at Truette and asked what brought him there and why was he riding on a horse with PG branded on it.

Truette, speaking in a very serious voice, very nervously told the evil old man he'd worked for PG Ranch many years ago, but had gone into the mountains looking for gold that he'd never found. Returning he'd found Mr. and Mrs. Randall dead at their ranch and that he had tried to work the ranch for a while, but the Indians had run him off. That's why he'd ended up where he now stood looking for a job. Hessenger looked into the eyes of Truette and saw death in them and knew right away that he was a hard man. The only job in town, he was told, was cleaning the stable. Cleaning the stable was a daily chore for Truette, but it was a must if he intended on finding out about the young girl. Standing at the entrance of the stable one day stroking his horse's mane, a buggy rolled into the stable with the most beautiful young girl on it along with a baby girl around three years of age. The young lady seemed to be too young to have such a child at that age, but the feeling within Truette's mind told the story of the young girls' past. Lowering his head as the young girl got off the buggy, the little girl spoke and told her mother, Catch me when I jump, Mommy. Both seemed so happy on the outside, but somehow the Cowboy wondered how the young girl really felt on the inside. Moving past the Cowboy, the little baby girl spoke again as she looked into Truette's eyes saying, Look, Mommy, the Cowboy's crying. The young girl asked the Cowboy if anything was wrong and the Cowboy shook his head no and took a step closer to them as he whispered that he had something private to tell her, but it wouldn't be smart to speak right now.

As Truette walked his horse away, the young girl noticed the PG brand on the horse's left rear side.

Many thoughts raced through the young girl's mind since PG was always used on her mother and father's ranch when she was young. Remembering the day when Hessenger and his gunmen had killed her family. The sounds rang over and over in her head of her little three-year-old brother as he'd been branded on the back and left for dead;

seeing her father's face when he'd been shot to death in front of her eyes as her mother was beaten and raped repeatedly by Hessenger's gunmen. Now out of nowhere, a cowboy was telling her she needed to know something, what could be so important after all these years, yet it puzzled her mind as well as her heart. Every day looking from a distance, Truette could only look at the young girl and her daughter before and after a buggy ride, which was the only place they were allowed to go...Under the watchful eyes of hired ruthless gunmen who would kill in a blink of an eye. As if killing was a game they played each, day, ordered to protect her or keep her prisoner for life to enjoy her as he pleased.

Time and time again the buggy rides took their place as the Cowboy waited with a small note to give the young girl, saying that many years ago, her mother Peggy Randalls had sent him a telegram that only said to come because she needed help...also that when he'd arrived everyone was dead and he buried them next to the grave marked PG. The note brought memories she wished never to come float in her mind. Back in her hotel room, behind closed doors, Sue Randalls cried out as her little baby girl slept peacefully. But now her name was Sue Randalls Hessenger because of the forced marriage the Hessenger arranged for her. Wiping away her tears, she could feel a small sense of new hope of having a chance to be free from the embrace of Hessenger s madness. Remembering all the times at night as she was being abused which led her to have the child who slept next to her side. Little Betsy, not knowing anything about her mother's past, believed she was happy because the small child could not see through the pretending faces that kept both of them safe and at harm's or death's path.

A very strong feeling began to subside in Sue's heart that she might be able to get away from Hessenger. But how or when would be an extremely difficult task due to the mob of gunmen always guarding the doors of her room as well as the whole town. Everything in the town belonged to Hessenger for many years. But the greed and cruelty displayed to any human being showed more and more each day. So it meant that at any time, if Hessenger would even think someone was up to undo any wish he demanded their life was on the line and death to anyone could be brought at the blink of an eye from the devil himself.

Not wanting to write a long note, Sue simply wrote that each day at the same time, a buggy ride was and had ever been the only time that she and her daughter were able to get out of her hotel room. The notes continued back and forth and on one certain day, Sue was to lure the buggy driver inside the stable so Bill Truette could knock him out and change clothes with him. They would ride off with the young girl and her baby daughter sitting quietly in the buggy - this was the only way out.

While waiting to make their getaway, the cowboy kept going to the hotel to eat and get a drink. Wanting to get closer to Hessenger,

Truette sat at the corner stool which was always empty. While the Cowboy was sitting there, one of the gunmen told him that no one sits there because the evil old man didn't want anyone sitting behind him. He was also told that Hessenger liked sitting where he could see out the windows, yet never with his back to a door.

Truette told the gunman to forgive him, but no apology could cure the bad thoughts Hessenger felt when someone disobeyed his wishes. As other gunmen got around the Cowboy, it seemed as if he'd been chosen to amuse the evil old man with violence as four gunmen began to beat Truette. Sue had been watching from the upper room where she had left the door cracked open to look downstairs as her baby girl slept peacefully in her room. Seeing Truette being beat down, she did something she'd never done before - she left her room and was standing next to the evil old man whispering something he did not care to hear, only that she had not gotten permission to step outside her room. The slap across Sue's face could be heard all the way across the first floor of the hotel as the gunmen stopped beating the Cowboy to see what had happened as Hessenger yelled at Sue I told you never to leave that room unless I say so...Holding her face as she got up after falling from the slap, she cried and looked at the Cowboy on the floor to let him know she had done it for him. Realizing how Sue had sacrificed herself for him, Truette had his hand on the butt of his gun ready to kill Hessenger, but as he looked around many gunmen were around to see all the commotion and there was no way to shoot all of them. If he could, it would be hard to get the girl and her baby out safely out of town because more gunmen awaited on the streets somewhere.

Quietly moving his hand away from his gun, the Cowboy stood up slowly walking outside as Sue went up the stairs into her room. Standing outside the window, Truette looked into the eyes of Hessenger, as the evil old man glanced back at him with a smirk and thought the Cowboy had been taught a lesson. Truette smiled back to fool the evil old man and leave it at that for now, but in his mind he vowed to kill the evil old man some day.

Stepping off the corner of the porch of the hotel Truette bumped into Mary Hagger from the general store. As their eyes met once more as before, something drew them closer as if a need to hold on to each other. Looking into her eyes, the cowboy asked if she was OK in this town. Other gunmen walking down the street told both of them to move on or else. Mary Hagger dropped her eyes as Truette promised her he would return to speak with her. Walking through the hotel doors, Mary Hagger made her way past the guards as if told what to do and it was only the orders of the evil old man that she was obeying. Which was to feed the young boy in the wine cellar below the hotel or die. Everyone knew Mary Hagger and what the evil old man had done to her husband many years ago, except for Truette.

CHAPTER 7

Back at the Indian camp the flaps from the tepee s entrance were being slowly opened as the warriors gathered around a fire that one of them had been chosen to keep a watch on and the fire was at full bloom. As the sun made its way across the morning sky the death of the four riders was to take place, but it had to be a slow painful death as each one of the remaining riders would watch and hear the other die. Dancing in a circle the young warriors' cries to the spirits began to take place as the riders watched from a distance with fear instilled into their bodies. Stopping only for moments at a time each one of the warriors rubbed the death paint onto their faces and bodies as the old miner rode his donkey closer to the Indian campfire. He stopped and told the four riders that only one a day was going to die and that it would be a very slow and painful death because of what they had done to the Cowboy's family. Looking into one of the four riders' faces, the young white warrior pointed as to show which one would be the first to die. The beating began with long switches that were wet to leave red bleeding streaks across the back of the one chose to die first. As the beating took its toll, the rider's yells echoed throughout the mountains, but no one would come to help. It was Indian land and not a white soul would even care to come so close, as The old miner was the only one to be allowed to go and come as he pleased. The other was Truette who was far away at the town that lay over the mountains. As the rider now began to pass out from pain, cold water would awaken him while being cut down from his bondage and taken out into the open fields where the blazing sun's light into the rider's face would burn the skin into one huge blister because melted animal fat was rubbed all over the body while tied down to spikes on the ground. With the sunrise to the back of the rider's head, having his eyelids sewn to his eyebrows would only make things worse as the sun would bake the body burning the eyes very slowly. Moving would tear the skin on his back as the rider laid on cactus and had urine poured on his body that would burn when the skin came open. As a rock was placed into the rider's mouth, he would be unable to spit it out for a leather strap had been tied around his head and in between his lips. This was to allow the earth worms in his nose to do as they pleased, moving slowly into the body.

While the other warriors rode their horses in a fast pace circling the rider's body, each one shot arrows into his arms and legs, not hitting his torso, allowing the rider to die of slow bleeding and pain. As the sun's light began to fade away, the dust from the body of the rider washed away, bound from his ankles and being dragged told the other three riders the first was dead or would be from being dragged across the river's cold water back and forth.

Riding past the three riders, the first rider was finally dragged away into the sunset. A meal was once more promised to the buzzards above as they flew in the direction of the dead body that would soon be cut down far away from the Indian camp. Walking up to the three remaining riders, the young white warrior once again pointed to another rider to let him know he was chosen next to meet a justice that only promised death - the way of life to any enemy of the Indian people.

More wood was added to the fire that would burn into the night; the old miner looked into the eyes of the riders asking them why they had done as they wished with the cowboy's family. Each tried to place the blame on each other, the old miner stood up and walked over to one of them, telling him it would do no good to blame someone else because the young white warrior had already chosen him to die next, smiling as he slapped him across the face. Walking over to the next one, he told him, tomorrow I'll slap you, OK? Standing near the last one without saying a word, the rider asked where the women and children were in hopes to get help, but the old miner could read the hopes coming from the rider and told him that this camp was not the real Indian camp, only a camp of young warriors between the real camp and the river. The women and children were moved to the back of the trees that outlined the land across the river and meadows until each rider had been put to death, when everyone would return close to the river again. The rider told the old miner that he didn't understand. The old miner smiled and told him, You must be the brains of the bunch, because the rider was not only trying to get into the old miner's mind, but into his heart in hopes of getting cut down and let go. Spitting into the face of the rider, the old miner told the story of how Indians believed that spirits roamed over the river's waters and the Indians killing each of the riders was to give the spirits a show of death. As death took its toll, the spirits would collect the dead riders' spirits as well as torture them even more. The Eyes of the rider showed more fear for he could see the old miner was not going to help or care to help any one of them. Walking away, the old miner told the riders not to worry that each one of them would die a different way because the young warriors did not want to bore the spirits of the Indian people. As he had laid out an old blanket next to the fire for the night, the donkey roamed but it would not go too far since the old miner was its only true friend. The young warrior who kept the fire burning sat at a distance sharpening a knife off a flint rock. The knife once belonged to one of the four riders, but now it was the fire keeper's.

Once again howls from a distance told of the wolves roaming the night, as Ring of Smoke, the baby wolf also howled his cries into the dark sparkling night. Truette had chosen to leave the baby wolf with the young white warrior, his nephew, but he only fed the wolf once and placed his hands on the wolf's head as to send a message into the mind of the wolf. The food, the touch, caring of having the little wolf around had seemed to sink into the baby wolf for it made its home next to the young white warrior's tepee as it rested for the night.

As the fire keeper slowly walked behind the riders to test and see if the knife could cut without the riders feeling it as they slept. It did not work as each rider flinched thinking it might be a bug bite, letting it go at that trying to get more rest. The knife would be used once the death of the second rider would take place.

One down, three to go. Soon, time took its toll all the riders would be dead and as the sun once again started to take its place in the morning sky; the young warrior had already been sitting behind the riders as the other warriors began to circle the fire. Walking past the rider which was chosen to die next, the young warrior stopped about three feet in front of the riders and spoke to the fire keeper in Indian language. The fire keeper stood up sticking the blade of the knife in the fire until it was red hot. Walking up to the white young warrior, he handed him the knife. The young white warrior slowly turned around looking at the riders with a smile which slowly faded away into a face of pure hate, his eyes needing to start the painful death. All this was too much for the fourth rider as he passed out thinking of dying any day now. Grabbing the second rider's hair from the top of his head, pulling upward as the knife cut through the layers skin close, very close to the bone of his skull as he yelled for help, the warriors let out howls into the morning skies calling the spirits in the cold river's waters to come soon to collect yet another evil soul. But it would be a while for the torture had just begun in the life of the second rider. Ring of Smokes' howls into the morning skies sent chills into the third rider's body as he watched the second rider being scalped right next to him. Only half his head had been scalped and sprinkled with dirt that would slow down the bleeding, but the pain would still remain as the rider was cut down and led over to the fire. The knife once again was plunged into the fire as the rider's eyelids were held open with the blazing red hot blade so close to his eye it burned away his vision bringing much pain into the life of a coward rider. He would not be put to death as the torture would continue.

Now on all fours crawling around, the rider was left alone as the warriors watched him fight for life. Once in a while the young white warrior brushed an arm or leg with a twig as the rider flinched thinking more pain would follow. Speaking again, the young warrior told the other Indians what he wished for them to do. Standing over the rider with long thin twigs soaked in water, they started whipping the rider's back as he yelled, crawling straight into the fire. Now that the pain was taking its toll as he jumped out of the fire and balled up yelling for help. Tying his ankles with a rope to be dragged slowly away into the pasture where more pain would be instilled into the rider until death would make its call. Slowly dragging the blind, scalped, whipped, fire-burnt rider would face even more torture, but he would be let out in the sun as the warriors would again shoot arrows into his arms and legs. He would be left alone to die or be eaten up by hungry predators like tiny little ants that would slowly eat away until nothing was left but bones. Buzzards and wild wolves would join in on the treat as the sun would again make its descent into another night.

From a distance the old miner's mind had drifted off into that dreadful night when Hessenger and his men had hurt him and left him for death to capture his soul. Also remembering how the Indian Chief and his people had saved his life. Now the young warriors who had been so young were torturing men. Though he had taught them a thing or two, it was nothing compared to the way they so naturally learned how to torture their enemy. So to be a friend was a reward in life as the touch of the white young warrior's hand upon the shoulder brought the old miner back from day dreaming as they both exchanged a smile and nod to assure a friendship would always be there; no matter what.

As the buzzard's trace disappeared in the late night sky, a new day would dawn of slowly killing the third rider with yet a different method of tormenting death. The sparkling stars once again danced in the dark pitch night as the old miner thought of his new friend Truette and what the cowboy might be doing. Sounds of howls coming from Ring of Smoke like an angel of the night had brought the old miner back to understand and hope everything would be OK. He then saw a falling star in the open sky as he made a wish to someday see his son again as he'd wished many, many nights before going to sleep.

The death of the third rider as the sun once again made its dance across the sky began with both his hands and ankles tied in a sitting position with a cat-tail shoot in his mouth. Rocks were placed in between his

45

legs so he could not move, but would be able to live if he was able to keep the cat-tail shoot in his mouth. The warriors swam by the rider under water as each stuck him with devil-head stickers that clung to animal fur. Then each warrior swam past him once again pulling at the fur quickly to cause pain hoping he would lose the grip of the cat-tail shoot causing him to drown in the water. Over and over the pain took its course until late in the afternoon. The rider was showing a strength to survive, yet death would and did take its toll as the warriors now shot arrows into the river while riding horses. It would only take one arrow and the rider would not be able to hold on to the cat-tail shoot as pain would shoot through his body.

This would cause him to let go; only living as long as he could hold his breath. Air bubbles coming to the surface of the river's cold water told he had almost given up as he tried to breathe through the cat-tail shoot while biting down on it. In moments the floating-away cat-tail shoot made its distance from the rider as more bubbles danced their way upward to the top of the river. Another endless fight for life had taken place as the fourth rider looked on with hope to live, yet death would soon begin for him when the sun would once again meet the sky.

The old miner looked on as the body was pulled out of the water with hands and ankles still tied together. Dragged past the fourth rider as the warriors' yells caused him to faint from terror of how the third rider looked to him. Laughing the old miner made his bed roll next to the fire for another night's rest. While Ring of Smoke sat next to the young white warrior's tepee showing to guard his friend inside while keeping an eye on the final rider seemed to be a sign that the little wolf knew the enemy even though the enemy was weak and hungry as well as tied spread eagle from tree to tree. The flames from the fire arose into the sunset as the fire keeper spent the night watching the fire as well as the fourth rider who would die the next day. From the reactions he showed crying and fainting, it wouldn't take much to bring the death that was promised to him.

The stillness of the night had caused the old miner not to sleep as he slowly crawled up to the fourth rider who was asleep. Gagging him with the fur filled with stickers, the fourth rider awoke to see the old miner shoving the fur into his mouth making it impossible to yell. His eyes told of the pain the stickers caused as the old miner stuffed it deeper and deeper into the back of the rider's mouth. Now no sound could be heard as the old miner pulled out his knife holding on to the rider's left thumb while cutting it completely off, knowing what kind of pain it had caused sent memories of that night Hessenger had cut off his trigger finger on both hands, after he was beat and left to die. Flashes of the night the Indian Chief stood over him helping him, for which he now owed the Indians his life.

Moments later as the old miner looked to see if anyone had noticed him, the fire keeper stood on the other side of the fire, the flames silhouetting his body. He looked at the old miner like he didn't even care if he killed the fourth rider. As Ring of Smoke also looked on with a howl into the late night darkness, the old miner smiled at the fire keeper as each went about as if nothing had happened.

The bleeding from the cut-off thumb ran down the arm and side of the body onto the leg of the rider until it made its way to the ground drying like caked mud. But this could only be seen when the sun made its way around once more.

Standing in front of the fourth rider who would be put to death, the young white warrior walked over to the fire keeper as he held out his hand for the knife which he placed over the fire until it was red hot. He went up to the fourth rider grabbing a- hold of his right thumb waking him with the red hot blade cutting his thumb cleanly off his hand. No sound could be heard, so the fur had to be pulled out to hear the cries of the coward rider again and again as each finger was sliced off one at a time. Then slowly making small cuts with the knife, the young white warrior motioned to the other warriors to beat the rider's arms and legs breaking all the bones to bring more pain. A rope was tied to the rider's ankles once again as he was dragged away full speed from the camp. It seemed that the Indian warriors knew that the fourth rider chosen had been the weakest and had to be put to death quicker or the fear and shock would win the battle of death the rider needed to have.

As the dust settled from the dragging body, all the riders were dead and women and children would move closer to the river as before. Making new friends, Ring of Smoke was the main attraction as the Indian children loved to play with him.

Ring of Smoke

CHAPTER 8

The echoes of drunken men yelling awoke Truette from another endless dream in which he'd been dancing with his wife Amy. As he shifted to one side looking out the hay loft window of the stable, straight ahead from the hotel he noticed that Hessenger and a bunch of his men had made two drunk cowhands fight each other in a brawl, where only one would be the survivor. For it was understood that it was a fight to the end, or get shot to death by the gunmen who stood at the ready to kill. As the people cheered them on, the evil old man had known how to use violence as a means to entertain the town for many years.

Looking on, Truette could only think of how to bring down Hessenger, yet it would take more than one to do so. No one could do it alone and live to see another day. Killing the evil old man would or was not a problem, but getting away alive would be, because the hired gunmen would shoot to kill as well. Besides Truette needed to get the young girl out of the embrace of danger which now seemed a way of life to her and her daughter. A few buildings away more people had showed up to see yet another night of violence which only spoke of how the evil old man had let his anger speak through the actions that were now displayed by a tremendous act of survival between two innocent drunk men. Within the crowd of people, Truette noticed a woman who stood slightly to the edge of the moonlight - Mary Hagger, the lady from the general store.

Quickly and very quietly, Truette slid out the window and off the roof of the stable. As he stood in the darkened shadows of the night, he knew that Mary Hagger would walk his way to go through the side door of the general store, where she lived as well. Then the sound of gun fire tore into the night once more. As Hessenger with a nod of his head had given orders to shoot the two men because it was taking too long to wait for a winner. Silence once more cleared the violent act of death as Hessenger spoke very loudly that next time he promised a better show ordering all the people back to their homes.

As Mary Hagger opened the door taking the keys out of the lock, it seemed as if in a split second her life would end. The force from the body behind her pushed at her while one hand was over her mouth and another held her tightly. But a gentle voice assured her that it was OK and that he meant no harm. Closing the door with the heel of his boot, Truette held on to her for a while as he spoke to her and told her he was the stranger in town who lived in the stable.

The shock and terror in Mary Hagger's body slowly began to clear away and being in the arms of a stranger somehow felt so safe. From the moment she had laid her eyes on Truette, she could tell the stranger in town was not at all like any man she'd known in a very long time.

Releasing her as he turned Mary Hagger around caused a feeling she had not had in a long time. But the gentleman that Truette was would be the only reason not to take advantage of her, and it sure was not the reason he'd wished to speak with her. Whispering in the dark, Truette told her that he would put his life on the line and ask her for a favor which was to send a telegram to his boss in another state asking for help, to please come quick. Asking no questions, Mary Hagger agreed as she stood in front of Truette in a daze and it took a while for each of them to realize danger loomed every moment in their lives. Opening the door once more, Truette would step out into harm's way as it now seemed to overshadow his life every day.

The next day would bring a new hope, the kind of hope that would get the young girl out of the danger she faced each day as well as the fear of losing her young daughter Betsy. Each day would start with a buggy ride which seemed to be the only time and place the young woman and child were allowed to go or do and it was to a special place with the scenery of snow-capped mountains. They sent the minds of both girls to dream on forever, or so it seemed. But Truette, who had not seen this place, would do so today as he had noticed the buggy driver limped with his left leg. He would come into the stable to set up the buggy for the morning ride out of town. Climbing onto the buggy, the limping driver rode across the street in front of the motel as the beautiful woman and her child got onto the buggy then rode out of town as two gun men on horseback would follow once the buggy rode past them. That day as the buggy driver limped into the stable. Truette knocked him out cold with an axe handle, took the limping buggy rider's clothes off and put them on himself, then slicing his throat as he covered the body under some hay. He very calmly and carefully limped out into the street with the buggy being pulled with only one horse. Climbing on the buggy as to ride it to the front of the hotel the two girls now awaited to get on. They sat quietly as before while the buggy driver slowly past the two gun men on their horses who were to follow in behind the buggy to guard the picnic that took place each day.

Having to speak to the young woman, Truette asked which way to go as he told her not to talk too loudly but to direct him which way he needed to drive. He advised her to remember when they arrived at the site of the picnic to have her daughter lie down on the ground and yell at the gun men that her little girl was hurt. Once the gun men's back was to Truette, he would have a chance to kill them both because face to face he would not.

The plan had worked as both gun men were new laid out dead with bullets in each from the gun of Truette. Throwing each of them on to the buggy and taking their horses would be much easier to get away with than to try and ride a buggy in the open rocky desert. Spooking the buggy's horse and sending it into the direction of the town would create a big surprise for all to see.

As a trail of dust was seen from a distance, the gun men sent word to Hessenger to come and look as the buggy made its way into town. Upon stopping the buggy the two gun men were taken out and onto the street while Hessenger yelled once more to instill greater fear into the people of the town to whom he often reminded it belonged to him. Speaking as he walked back and forth in front of the gathering crowd, he promised that if anyone knew about this to step up now or later die for not letting him know.

More yells were heard that seemed more like a human barking orders to his men to not just stand around but to get ready to ride out and find out where the woman and child were as well as bringing them back along with the buggy driver.

Mounting up to ride out of town with some of his men, Hessenger vowed to return to punish anyone who knew anything about the incident. Following the trail of the buggy, it came to a stop at the few trees out in the open desert where he used to allow Sue and little Betsy a chance to get away as the view of the snow-capped mountains gave them another hope to someday become free from the evil old man. And that day had finally come true or for the moment it seemed that way. As the evil old man looked beyond the few trees, he could see that the trail of his two gun men's horses led into the direction of the mountains. As he and his men followed it, he would come to a stop in only a few moments as he witnesses hundreds of hoof prints which made it impossible to know exactly where and in which direction they would lead him. Taking another glance the evil old man could see a wide band of Indian warriors lined up across an opening into the mountains ordering his men to stop, taking a deep breath as he once again spoke very slowly that he would not risk his life for the young girl or his little daughter. From the coldness in the sound of his voice as he spoke to his men, they could tell what type of man he really was and that he really didn't care for Sue or little Betsy. As he slowly turned his horse around and motioned to his men that it was not time to go back.

Riding back to town had given Hessenger time to wonder if Sue had any feelings for him while he smiled on in a mocking way. Yet he was now wondering about his little Betsy who he'd never taken the time to play with not even once. For all he ever cared about was how much he could gain for nothing and just end up taking anything he could call his own. Paying his men had led up on each receiving a part of land or business in town which at any given moment in time even his own men would end up dying if another young gun could hold up to his test. A test where he called all the shots and to pass each would have to be very quick with a gun. They also would kill at a nod from his command. As he and his bunch grew into savage killers, Oakwood had provided a place to grow even larger and with the gold rush taking its toll in the mountains, anyone with it had ended up dead somewhere with no trace of gold at all. With Sue now gone, who could or would take the place of her? A prisoner to his every need of lust had turned Sue into a very strong woman who had kept so many years behind closed doors yet now was gone from his embrace where she would never again have him lust over her young soul and little Betsy was the only reason Sue really cared to live. As Hessenger neared the town, he could only wonder why the buggy driver had betrayed him and if he ever got a chance he promised to kill him on the spot.

As the hot sun beamed down on Hessenger and his men, beads of sweat rolled down their faces. For the first time in his life, Hessenger slowly let out some tears in a moment when he let himself slip away from his wicked ways because he was now thinking of how it would have been to just be a normal man.

Then a breeze of wind caught his attention as he held up his head and hoped no one had noticed the tears in his eyes. Acting as if he were wiping away the sweat from his face, he ran his handkerchief across his brow to erase the emotion that had taken place for a brief moment. Beyond the town's entrance, Hessenger and his men could see a crowd forming in the middle of the street right in front of the Stable as some of his men were dragging a body from inside the stable, which revealed to be the real buggy driver. Dismounting his horse, the evil old man spoke to his men and the townspeople that no one was to step onto the streets of Oakwood until he ordered it was OK. While still speaking, Hessneger walked past the stable onto the edge of town as he looked up until he could see the gun men. On top each stood looking back at him, one of each side of the street's buildings. Puzzled, they began to glance at each other and before their eyes could look back down at the evil old man; bullet pierced each one's heart. In only a split second the bodies crumpled down the side of the buildings. The evil old man seemed to be getting old, but the speed of guns being drawn appeared to not slacken up. Slowly turning around and reloading his own 45's never looked back up at anyone, he spoke that when a guard failed to do his job, he would kill him on the spot. It had been plain to see that the two guards on top of the buildings had let the Cowboy ride out right front of their faces. Ordering two more men to watch anything going or coming, he stated that they had better not go to sleep until their replacements took turns.

Stopping on the steps of the hotel, Hessenger turned around speaking once more saying, I promised a better show and there you have it, now listen and listen good, Oakwood belongs to me, I do as I please and you do as I say or else, now get out of here and crawl back into your mouse holes, the show is over...

Not wanting to be seen, Mary Hagger looked through the windows of the general store wondering if the evil old man would find out that she had sent out a message for Truette. That alone would cause her to be killed and as the thoughts lingered in her mind, she honestly knew the answer, but the hope of what the strange cowboy had told her that he would return again made it easier not to give up. For it seemed that Truette in her eyes was an honest cowboy and very much different to her than any man she'd known or seen in a very long time.

Going up to his room up the stairs would not be as before since his wife and child wouldn't be waiting this night. Another night in Oakwood had left men dead and the following morning wasn't promised to any of Hessenger's men, let alone the people who lived there who wished to get away from him. Armed men days and nights took turns with more careful watch for the example that had taken place was the only promise anyone would receive. Death was the penalty if anyone would not do as the evil old man had ordered in the town

Harold Datson, Jr. sat in the wine cellar wondering why Mary Hagger hadn't shown up with supper and news of the events that had taken place in Oakwood that day. But each time Mary had dropped by for a meal and to clean up, she had always brought more than enough, as Jr. pondered while he was now enjoying his left overs.

Oakwood would soon become known but not the way Earl Hessenger had ever planned. For the killings that had taken place would be the reason someone would stop his ways. And the only one who could stop him would be Bill Truette "The Cowboy". But alone he had no chance. He'd vowed to come back for the evil old man to clean up the town of Oakwood. Having met Mary Hagger had made it a must to come back since she had risked her life for him sending out that telegram. In her room at the general store, she lay down to go to sleep and in the midst of the night's silence, she could hear footsteps on the wooden porch of the store. But as before, for many years it had been the armed guards who belonged to Hessenger. She would never forgive him because many years ago her husband had died in the middle of the street which had just become a small town as several men had arrived to take it over. Standing alone in the street, Mary's husband had been the only man to face Hessenger. In her mind she could still see Hessenger and his men getting off their horses. They formed a line across the street and each drew their guns quickly all at once. No words were spoken until her husband laid down dead, stepping out of the line of men, Earl Hessenger loudly and very boldly said that this small town would be his from now on. He also told them that if anyone had a word to say about it to step up now or never disrespect his wishes or else. In moments she had fallen to sleep as before, but this time, a new hope to see the stranger once more was her new prayer.

CHAPTER 9

Riding away from Hessenger was the first time Sue had ever tried to get away. It meant she could not be caught because of the way Hessenger dealt with anyone that had tried to escape. Death or a punishment that made her wish she was dead was the price to pay for disobeying his wishes. The baby girl Betsy in the saddle with Truette sat safely and holding onto him made the cowboy smile as they rode into the mountains.

From a distance on the smaller mountain tops held a silhouette of many Indian warriors lined up ready to ride down in the direction of the cowboy to lead him into safety. Yelling to her uncle, Sue told him that up ahead were many Indians as the cowboy's smile would tell a story of his new friends. As he spoke to Sue and the little girl Betsy, he told them that they were his friends, which was extremely rare in this land of many Indians.

There was renewed hope of safety and her mind was more at ease for the moment. Like a stampede of wild horses, the Indians rode down the mountains as they made howling noises that echoed into the mountains and beyond- The young girl and her baby had never ventured out of town as far as they were now, only when she had been abducted from her parents' ranch which brought the memories back to float to the top of her mind causing fear to raise chills all over her body. The baby girl's eyes Widened as the Indians passed by to see if anyone might have been on their trail.

Speaking to the little baby girl, Truette said it would be OK and soon they would rest in a peaceful place. The ride back to the Indian camp would take a while as the young warriors on bareback horses were used to such things and in time it seemed as if each one would be doing tricks on the horses to make the little girl laugh, but soon she would tire and fall asleep in the cowboy's arms. As Truette glanced back at the young girl, his smile reassured his niece that the embrace of the evil old man was not a concern any more and that a new life laid ahead. What kind it would be puzzled her innocent mind.

With the Indian camp coming into view, a mist of tepees outlined the landscape on the other side of a river that seemed to be used to hold off traffic from coming at full speed, but also warning crossers to enter at one's own risk. Crossing to the other side was like entering into another world as the warmth of the campfires gave a feeling that assured the body something would protect it and there was food all around. Young Indian children ran close to see the riders approach the camp as some pointed to the little blond girl with a smile. New friends had been made at a glance, but only for the Indian children because Betsy had never seen any small children running around playing who were her age.

From the side of the horse, Betsy sat with the Cowboy looking up ahead at one small Indian girl who waited for them to come closer tossing a rag doll into the air. The Cowboy caught it with one hand and gave it to little Betsy. The little rag doll wore a headband of beads that were the colors of light green turquoise and the blood red ruby beads stood out the most. They seemed to Him that it pointed to the four corners of the world: north, south, east and west. The let black hair on the rag doll could have meant midnight, for each thing the Indian people made had a meaning.

The Cowboy then looked back where the little Indian girl had stood but she was no longer in sight. Like a spirit she had vanished so fast. Looking back at the little rag doll, the Cowboy noticed a silhouette of a wolf on the doll's dress and he was reminded of Ring of Smoke. This sent his eyes roaming around trying to find his baby wolf. At the exact same spot the little Indian girl had stood when she tossed the doll was Ring of Smoke. Turning his horse around the Cowboy, now puzzled, got off his horse and knelt down on one knee calling out for his friend to come to him. Betsy now stood next to Truette looking on as her eyes widened as they had when she saw the Indian warriors for the first time.

Holding her close, the Cowboy told Betsy it was OK and that the little wolf's name was Ring of Smoke. Jumping up into the Cowboy's arms, Ring of Smoke licked his face letting his friend know how much he'd missed him. Letting little Betsy pet the wolf brought the biggest smile on her face she had ever had in her life and the Cowboy could tell it was a happy moment she would never forget.

A few feet away stood the huge Indian Chief whose eyes could easily reveal a welcoming smile to the Cowboy and little Betsy. Then a moment of silence took place as he walked up to Sue as tears began forming in his eyes. The Cowboy knew he had made a friend, not only in the time of need, but with a heart of gold. Next to the Indian Chief stood the old miner holding on to his whiskey bottle while his donkey roamed freely amongst the tepees. Stepping out of the Indian Chief's tepee, the young, white, blue eyed, long blond haired warrior stood looking at his sister for the first time since the evil old man Earl Hessenger had turned their world upside down

Only one look and Sue knew her little brother Bobby was still alive running to him with open arms, he did the same for her. As Sue spoke to Bobby, tears rolled out of her eyes, but the young warrior did not understand what his Sister was saying because he only spoke the language of the Indians since he'd lived and learned their ways. But Bobby knew that Sue was his sister because the Indian Chief had told him and cowboy the story of their life with the help from the old miner who stood there with tears in his eyes as well. Speaking to the old miner, the Indian Chief could see a new look in his eyes for his old friend had no secrets to hide from him. Each spoke to tell the cowboy to stay at the camp until it was safe for all of them. The young girl Sue and her little baby Betsy were safe now as Bobby the young warrior knelt in front of his niece smiling and giving her a big hug with the old miner standing next to them, speaking to Sue and Betsy with a huge toothless grin, saying, WELCOME HOME MY FRIENDS.

Sleeping in a tepee was different for the young girl and her daughter, but it seemed so right and most of all safe from the embrace of Hessenger. A new day promised a new beginning as the Indian Chief and his people lived for happiness and cared for each other. Walking around the Indian camp, Sue and her baby Betsy seemed at home, but they needed a place. Not only a place, a place where they could call home to grow up and live a normal life.

The sound of the Cowboy's voice brought a smile to both as he spoke of living at the PG ranch which wasn't too far from the Indian camp across a few hills. The same river passed by each place.

Riding horses, each one pointing out different places or new discoveries, the young girl and her daughter smiled at each other and to the Cowboy who was next to the young warrior. The moment of silence took place as the PG ranch came into focus, but the cowboy broke the silence saying that everything would be OK from now on and that he would never leave their sight, so help him God.

Standing outside the gate to the ranch, the Cowboy put an arm around

Sue as he held little Betsy in his other arm. Sue was shaking in fear as she remembered how many years ago her mother and father Peggy and Jake Randalls had died from the evil old man's ways. Holding each other tight, the Cowboy promised a new life for both as Ring of Smoke ran past them into the ranch.

They all laughed out loud watching the little wolf as he had kept the emotions from taking control as he howled inside the ranch claiming his new home to protect.

The first step into the gates of the ranch, a whisper in the wind of Sue's mother brought tears to form on the edges of her eyes as she could still hear her mother tell her to promise not to tell anyone about the gold. In a short distance the old miner had been riding behind the Cowboy as thoughts began to swim in his mind of years ago. A secret he never told anyone except the Indian Chief.

Day dreaming about his younger days without the need to drink his memories away made him take a big swig from his whiskey bottle. Barely able to hold it with one hand, most fingers were nubs after the second joint. They had been cut off, not from an accident, but from a sharp knife. Held down on his wooden porch steps to the ranch house, two men beat him as the same evil old man who'd killed the cowboy's sister and brother-in-law took young Sue who was before him now. The long-kept secret of having been left to die and unable to use his hands again as he once had with a gun, his memories took over and he let his donkey wander slowly away from the trail, the old miner now deep within his daydream, still lived to somehow get even with the evil old man in town, but how? The secret he had held on to for so many years required answers, especially what had happened to his then ten year old son who was taken by the evil old man. By now he would be twenty two if still alive, a young man somewhere. At one point in time, the old miner had been fast with a gun and the evil old man, Earl Hessenger in Oakwood had heard of his talents wanting to buy his services. Not wishing to go see what the evil old man wanted had caused an anger in the evil old man to come in the middle of the night kicking in the doors of the old miner's home cutting off the fingers of his hand so he could not use a gun a- gain. Being beaten half to death didn't allow him to follow where they had taken his son. Besides, a threat of death had been whispered into his ear not to follow or the boy would surely die.

Two years after the evil old man's ordeal with the old miner was about the time when the cowboy's sister and brother-in-law had their dreams ripped away as well. Retreating into the mountains ashamed of not being able to help his own son, the old miner never returned to his own ranch. But his young son had been taken into Oakwood, Hessenger's town. Imprisoned in the wine cellar, he was held in this dungeon and not allowed to the light of day. Three times a day, Mary Hagger from the general store, whose husband had lost his life to the evil old man, was ordered to feed the boy. As years went by, a lantern was the only light he'd known. As a cruel joke, a gun without bullets and the hammer removed along with an old piece of rope on a holster was tossed into the wine cellar. Let's see if you can get as fast as your father was the punch line. Mary Hagger was allowed to clean up after the boy who stood in a trance day in and day out, drawing the gun from the holster as if it would really work. Twelve years of the same old thing had made the boy lightning fast, creating a gunman, not knowing the evil old man had thrown in the rusted gun, holster and rope as a joke. Many knew of the boy in the wine cellar, as knew of the young girl Sue who mothered a child Betsy from the evil old man. But the fear of speaking out had stopped anyone from doing anything about it or die as the evil old man had hundreds of men guarding the town of Oakwood.

Drifting away the donkey stopped walking and brought the old miner back to reality as he turned the donkey around in the direction of the PG ranch.

The Cowboy spoke only when he knew it was the right time a conversation should take place. Years of wisdom to know something was wrong always seemed to hold a silence only he could use himself. Stepping onto the porch, the old miner took a deep breath because the girl was safe back in her home and little Betsy made all the difference in the world. As the Cowboy walked past the old miner, he looked into his eyes and told him that if he ever needed to talk that his secret would be kept. Thanking the Cowboy, the old miner told Truette he had every right to know everything because it had happened to him as it did to the PG ranch. With a puzzled look, The Cowboy could feel that Hessenger and his gunmen had to be brought down, but death had to be the only way.

The first night no one could sleep because of all the planning that had to done in order to get the ranch running again. The chimney held a warm glow as Sue looked at the cowboy with a smile.

A tear began to roll down her face hugging her little Betsy, who was holding her rag doll. Bobby and the little wolf Ring of Smoke slept outside on the porch for the night had been beautiful. Rolling a cigarette, Truette wondered what had happened to the old miner, but for now his new friend would be OK. Closing his eyes, the cowboy once again seemed to begin dreaming of the moment he'd passed through Crystal Pit Canyon and Devil's Din Desert.

How his wife Amy had given birth to Patty Ann, then at PG ranch, Bob and Jerry were born. Life didn't seem fair, but what he'd done for Sue and little Betsy as well as for Bobby the young Indian warrior. Things would come to unfold as a family once more.

As the heat from the cigarette awoke him, the Cowboy tossed it into the fireplace as he rubbed his face with two hands. Tired he leaned back into the rocking chair and dozed off into a very deep sleep.

Ring of Smoke

The smell of coffee brewing and breakfast cooking awoke the Cowboy and Sue while the old miner, little Betsy, the Indian warrior Bobby and\ Ring of Smoke were all in the kitchen ready to eat. The old miner's voice told the Cowboy and Sue it was about time they got up. The ride had been a long one from the moment they'd gotten away from town and each one had not wanted to fall asleep too long out of fear of the evil old man. But once they were at PG ranch, it was a little different and more relaxing than the nights before. The happy faces of everyone in the kitchen brought joy to Truette's heart, but would not erase what had happened or how it made him feel.

After breakfast the old miner went outside to his donkey as the Indian warrior, little Betsy and Ring of Smoke followed behind. Inside Truette and Sue stood, promising to stay and fix up PG ranch as their new home. Unrolling his bedroll, Truette placed the branding iron, spurs and gun with holster over the fireplace as each had the letters "HD" on them.

CHAPTER 10

Each morning Truette awoke as the dawn's sunlight barely peeped over the mountain tops. Sitting in an old oak wood rocking chair with the letters "JR" which meant his brother-in-law had made it. Now it belonged to the Cowboy, as well as PG ranch. Cleaning the graves became routine and paying his respects was always the first thing after a moment in the rocking chair as he glanced out into the open meadows in search of anyone who may be coming his way. Raking dead leaves and releasing tumble weeds out into the open fields, he said a special prayer at the PG grave. In His mind whoever PG had been, his sister and brother-in-law had used their letter as an honor.

The sound of a cracking twig made the Cowboy spin around with his hand on the butt of his gun, but his eyes rested on Sue and he let go very slowly letting her know to please never sneak up on him again. Taking a few more steps, Sue asked why he had been speaking to the PG grave. The Cowboy told her that PG must have been a good person to her parents because those initials were used to name the ranch - a prestigious honor. Sue smiled at her uncle the Cowboy as she told him that the day Hessenger and his gun men had taken her away. She was only six and her mother Peggy had made her promise not to ever tell anyone about the grave. But as Sue now looked at her uncle Truette she could only say that it wasn't a person or an animal, or that it wasn't any type of bones. So if he wanted to know, he would have to dig it up. Intrigued, the Cowboy looked at Sue for a moment.

She spoke again saying that her promise to her mother would be kept and she would never tell. As tears rolled down her face, she told him that the reason her mother sent the telegram was because what was in that grave and that it belonged to him.

When her mother sent the telegram, they didn't have trouble. It came the day when her father went to town that was owned by Hessenger and his hired gunmen.

Now Truette needed to find out why this grave had been used to name the ranch as well as the livestock on it. Digging didn't take the Cowboy long to find the answer as he couldn't believe his eyes with all the gold he was digging up. Glancing up at Sue, the Cowboy told her that he now understood that PG stood for "Pure Gold". That was why his sister didn't say gold on the telegram she sent him. Turning around as he looked into the direction of the mountains, the Cowboy told her that in those mountains many had lost their lives looking for gold and down below where they now stood, some had lost their lives as well. Turning back to look at Sue, he told her that the choice would be hers to make: hide the gold forever or use it as she wished.

Sue spoke after a moment of silence that the gold by right belonged to the Indian Chief and his people. As another twig snapped behind them, they both turned to see who it was. The old miner had heard both of them talking and now was looking down at the grave with the gold nuggets in it. Looking at Sue and the Cowboy, he stood for a moment in shock walking past both of them, he said you do have a heart of gold and I as well will honor as you please. Lost in thought, he once again began to think of the night when he'd seen Hessenger took the girl into town and how for many years she had held the promise she kept for her mother. Wiping away tears, he motioned to them that breakfast was ready. And he promised not to say a word.

All the gold in the world could never buy the happiest little girl who was waiting in the kitchen with the young warrior and Ring of Smoke who sat next to her chair. Sue knew that the gold could and would bring trouble, but the look the Cowboy gave her read her thoughts somehow and she knew he would do the right thing.

After breakfast, the Cowboy loaded up the wagon with the gold and covered it up with a blanket. He told everyone that it was time to pay a visit to their friends, the Indian Chief and his people.

The Indian Chief sat on the ground by a campfire as he seemed to know the Cowboy was coming. As the wagon came to a stop, Ring of Smoke ran next to the Indian Chief because he held a piece of meat for him. Bobby the young warrior jumped off and motioned for little Betsy to jump as he caught her in midair and spun her around in a circle while she held onto her rag doll. Putting little Betsy down the Indian children ran to her with big smiles as she took off with them running to play. Sue was helped off the wagon by the Cowboy and the old miner got off the back of the wagon, walking straight to the campfire where more food would be. Truette walked over to where the Indian Chief was and sat next to him. The Cowboy spoke to him with the old miner translating about the gold which was rightly his to have and do as he pleased. As the old miner spoke to the Chief, he pointed to the sky watching the Eagle Pass by. As he spoke, the old miner translated his words saying that the shadow of the eagle had left a sign of more trouble to come to his people if the gold was to stay in the hands of his people. Pointing to little Betsy, the Indian Chief mentioned that it all would be better to find a way that it could belong to her for she was to be the chosen one between good and bad. After a brief pause, the Indian Chief spoke to the old miner. Not wanting to translate the words, he looked up hoping he would see the eagle return to change the Indian Chief's mind, but it was no where in sight.

Then slowly speaking to the Cowboy, he told him of the Indian Chief's plan to bring down Hessenger in town by using the old miner as bait. Only a piece of gold the size of an eye would be needed to capture Hessenger's attention as the cowboy was to go somewhere alone and bury the gold so no one would know, only him. The Indian Chief motioned to Truette to leave at once so he could go hide the gold then walked up to the wagon picking up a piece of gold that he tossed to the old miner to use as bait. The Indian Chief spoke more words to the old miner as Truette told Sue and little Betsy he would return soon. Riding away Truette would have to go hide the gold somewhere no one would know about. The secret of not telling anyone about the gold Sue kept quiet about for so many years was now in the hands of Bill Truette as he rode away on the wagon to bury the gold.

Three days had passed as Sue's face revealed a sign of relief as her uncle rode back into the Indian camp with a secret no one knew but him. The gold was once more buried somewhere, but this time the burden wasn't on Sue. Staying at the Indian Chief's camp a few more nights was to show him respect by getting to know of his people as they danced around a huge campfire calling the spirits to come forth from the nearby river. Looking into the cowboy's eyes, the Indian Chief gave him a smile as the Cowboy drew on the ground to let the Chief know where the gold was. Both grinned at each other for the gold meant nothing to either of them, but the secret was now more important yet so simple that they laughed out loud while everyone looked at them. Erasing the marks on the ground, the Cowboy laughed even harder as his friend the Indian Chief pointed to a falling star. Ring of Smoke howled into the night as everyone stopped to see the falling star disappear in midair. The dancing continued while the old miner stood at a distance with so many thoughts going through his mind. Wondering if his son could still be alive somewhere. As more memories touched his mind of how and when he'd come to this territory, he glanced towards the snow-capped mountains where he d been so many times looking for gold and how gold didn't matter as much as trying to outwit Hessenger and his hired gunmen, to bring them all to a stop.

In doing so, his life would be the one that might not make it back, but it was the only way anyone had ever tried to do so and, in fact, it was the only time anyone would stand against Hessenger and his ruthless killers in Oakwood, the town Hessenger had claimed his own many years ago.

The old miner had never sold out his guns and he sat wondering how it might have been to sell them out to Hessenger when he was asked to come work for him. But the use of his guns was a trademark of honesty and helping those in need, not to kill for pleasure or to take away land someone owned, especially going into Oakwood to take it over. The thoughts of how Sue's parents were murdered brought tears to his eyes because if he'd taken the evil old man's offer, it might have meant that he was chosen to kill Peggy and Jake Randalls with his own gun from orders from Hessenger and no telling how many more would and did get killed. What hurt more was the thought of not being able to help his own son being taken away from him the night Hessenger had come calling in the middle of the night to turn his world upside down forever. Going to town with a piece of gold as bait was no problem getting out alive was another story. He was glad he could finally get even with the evil old man. But if the bait didn't work, the old miner would die on the spot.

Looking back at the others at the campfire, the old miner walked over to Sue telling her she was the bravest young lady he'd ever met and that her daughter Betsy was the prettiest child he'd ever laid his eyes on. As Sue looked into the old miner's eyes, she could sense the fear within his soul, but she told him he was the bravest old man she had ever spoken to because no one else would risk their life to do what he was about to do for everyone.

The old miner pointed to the Cowboy and said, Now there's the bravest man I'd ever known because he'd walked into Oakwood with nothing to offer Hessenger like the piece of gold he had as well as the story of more gold that laid in wait to be his.

Sitting nearby, the Cowboy glanced over at Sue as she told the old miner that both of them were very special to her, then she smiled back at her uncle Bill. Keeping the secret about the gold had been kept for over ten years as Sue had promised not to tell. But now the gold had been reburied, it had only been three days when the Cowboy drew on the ground letting the Indian Chief know where the gold was. But for some reason, Sue knew it would be safe as she looked at both of her friends.

As the night grew darker, each one found a place to sleep while Ring of Smoke sat next to the fire keeper. On bareback horses three young warriors rode by the fire and out of sight keeping an eye out for trouble in case it came calling that night.

Truette rolled out his blanket, next to the wagon after he placed big rocks in front and back of the wheels so it wouldn't roll away. The cowboy began thinking of his wife and children as usual while he rolled a cigarette. Missing them had brought tears to his eyes and somehow it had to be a must to keep Sue, her girl Betsy, and Bobby the Indian Warrior safe. Together as a family for they were all he had left in this life. Earl Hessenger had to be stopped, but killing him would take more than one. As he placed his head on his saddle for a nights rest, he noticed the old miner fiddling with the piece of gold and a bottle of wine in his other hand. He wondered if it would be safe sending the old miner alone into Oakwood. Realizing no one else could go because for anyone else it would be death on the spot, he could only smile at the old miner and roll over for the night to pass.

Sounds of the old miner yelling and screaming at Ring of Smoke as he ran after him woke everyone up, because the wolf had the piece of gold in his mouth and the old miner was too slow to catch Ring of Smoke. After a good laugh, the baby wolf dropped the gold nugget and ran over to the Cowboy. As the old miner picked up the gold nugget, everyone laughed at him because he was still a little drunk.

Before heading back to the ranch everyone said their goodbyes and gave big hugs to each other. Bobby the Indian warrior spoke to the other warriors and some began to get ready to ride out with them.

The ride back to PG ranch took a few hours as everyone got off the wagon. Ring of Smoke took off after a rabbit next to the ranch, but the rabbit was too fast. But the ritual of being in control of the area was beginning to take place in the life of Ring of Smoke. Marking his territory by urinating on trees or bushes took place each time the chance came about. Only the Cowboy knew what the baby wolf was doing and in time others of the same kind would come calling to see if Ring of Smoke would go with them, or fight them off his land. Time would bring the answer, but the Cowboy would honor it if the little wolf decided to leave. But by the looks of things, PG ranch was Ring of Smoke's home and little Betsy was always playing with him.

Standing outside on the porch, Truette looked into the mountains wondering if the message to his boss had made it because he would never have a chance against Hessenger and his men. Inside the ranch, everyone relaxed and got a bite to eat as the fireplace provided light inside. The old miner took a look at the gun, spurs, and branding iron with the letters HD, getting lost in thought for a while wondering how and why had such things ended up at the PG ranch, but he didn't say a word. He only walked outside for a breath of fresh air and a big drink from his bottle to ease his mind.

The cowboy could tell something was on the old miner's mind, but he also knew that a man in thought would be better left alone to work out his own problems.

Building a small campfire, some young warriors stayed close to PG ranch in case help was needed for they would honor Bobby's wishes to assist them if it came down to it. Bobby, the young white warrior, had become more than a son to the Indian Chief.

He had begun to speak for the Indian Chief as if he would be the Chief and someday it would be him ruling and protecting his people with wisdom and respect for it would be an honor to fulfill and payback because his life had been saved when Bobby was only three years old. As Hessenger and his men had left him to die alone with a burn on his back from the PG branding iron, Bobby was alive and very strong. Getting even with Hessenger would become his most wanted wish in life and that time was almost near. In fact Sue's wish was the same for what Hessenger had done to her and her family.

CHAPTER 11

The keys to the wine cellar door awoke Harold Datson Jr. up as the lady from the general store Mary Hagger continued to do as ordered or die. And it was to take good care of the young man that was captive. After Harold Datson Sr. had refused Hessenger's wishes to work for him. After all these years had gone by, Mary Hagger never knew of the talents the young man's father had with guns, nor did she know how the young man had gotten there because he never spoke of his father or anyone else to her. But now he appeared to be very quick with a gun himself. But the gun had no hammer or bullets and in the young man's mind, the gun really worked as he acted like he was killing someone each day that passed.

Sitting down the basket of food and beginning to speak of the daily events in Oakwood. Mary Hagger would be the eyes of the young man as she would always tell him to have faith of someday stepping out into the streets. As she began telling the story about the cowboy in town and how he'd helped the young girl and her baby escape the embrace of the evil old man, she was reminded of how many times the thought of doing so herself, but the only reason she never did so was because of not wanting to leave the young man alone as she always tried to teach him a thing or two.

Ring of Smoke

The young man Harold Datson Jr. vowed each day that he would someday get his chance to kill Hessenger and a bunch of his men. Then the flashes in his mind of his own father's screams at night when his fingers had been cut off made him stand straight up pulling the gun without bullets in and out of the holster again and again killing unseen men around him. Alone in the wine cellar, the young boy had grown into a man and was now lightning fast with the gun if he ever got the chance to get his hands on a real one to kill with. He would ask Mary Hagger to bring him one all the time. But the fear Hessenger had instilled in her so many years ago forbid her to even think to try such a foolish thing.

If caught, she would die on the spot, just like her husband had paid with his life in the middle of the streets of Oakwood. Remembering that ominous day caused tears to flow out of her eyes as she sat in the wine cellar with nothing left to live for except the young man who now and as long as she could remember wanted to kill not only one man, but each and everyone who worked for Hessenger. Promising to return once again, she hugged the young man, but he would never look into her eyes.

Walking back to the general store, Mary Hagger noticed a line of people going into the saloon one at a time, but it appeared that all of them were women. The knowing nudge of a pistol poking her ribs along with an order to get in line with the rest of women persuaded her to participate in some kind of audition. The side door of the saloon had never been used, but they all were using it that night. The room was huge and lit up with lanterns as all the women were lined up along the walls for the evil old man Earl Hessenger was picking who was going to take Sue's place for his illicit pleasures. There was no question that the youngest and prettiest would be picked, but looking into the eyes of Mary Hagger, Hessenger spoke softly to her that if he hadn't chosen her to take care of the boy, she would be his right now as he touched her face. Mary Hagger pulled back. In all the years of giving orders to her, she had never resisted because he'd never touched her in any way. He only barked out orders to her to take care of Harold Datson Jr. or die. Pulling back had made the evil old man furious because his men were watching and laughed out loud when she did. Taking a step closer to Mary Hagger, he slapped her to the ground which made all his men stop laughing, as he yelled at her to get the hell out of his face. He then pulled out his gun and shot one of his own men between the eyes who was about 15 feet away and quickly put the gun back into his holster. To shoot his own man was to send out a message not to play any kind of games or laugh at him. Mary Hagger had gotten off lightly with only a slap. Grabbing a young girl by the arm and taking her away let everyone know he had made a choice of who would take Sue's place. Hessenger had always said that if a woman was given orders and she complied, nothing else would happen to her. Mary Hagger always did as she was ordered which was to take good care of Harold Datson Jr. But if she ever failed, she would fall prey to any one of Hessenger's men, or even himself. She had to be careful now because all the men thought she was no longer liked, but everyone was afraid of Hessenger, so no one bothered her at all.

Mary Hagger was safe to come and go as she pleased with the keys to the wine cellar dangling at her side. After Hessenger had made his choice and left, the other gunmen took out the one who was killed and grabbed a woman of their own to do with as they pleased as their husbands watched from the windows of their places. Mary Hagger laid alone in the dark crying as she always did, but this night was different because she was slapped across her face, but could have very well been shot to death. Oakwood was getting out of hand and all the men were too scared to even be seen together. Then the Cowboy came to her mind of how gentle he had held her in his arms as his low soft voice echoed in her mind. Oh, where could Bill Truette be right now and would she ever see him again?

Once again the morning sun told her she had made it to another day. The night's sounds of men going wild had lasted a very long time. One by one the women walked back to their homes as their husbands opened the doors to let them in. Some fell to their knees crying as their husbands helped them up. Others would push their husbands away not from a lack of love, but they felt filthy smelling like sweaty drunken gunmen. The sound of a shotgun had brought everyone out into the streets as one woman shot her husband, then herself.

Opening the general store daily wasn't fun anymore and everything sold or traded had to be reported to Hessenger since he owned all the main businesses in Oakwood and anyone passing through would never leave again. Oakwood once had a sheriff, but when the evil old man and his men rode into town, the sheriff just sat around too scared to do anything and in a very short time, he became one of Hessenger's gunmen, or he would die as many had before.

A storm loomed over Oakwood late into the night and the rain poured heavily for hours as the lightning flashes lit up the town but it meant that the roar of thunder would follow. The noise was loud and at times didn't match the lightning flashes before it. Something else was going on. The glowing eyes in the windows above her bed sent chills to Mary Hagger's body for it was not a white man and even if it was, the fear of being alone was just as bad. She could tell it was an Indian warrior with a painted face.

Her husband told her about two white stripes across the face and over one eye. It would be a message or a sign she would soon come to know.

The usual morning rush to and from each place everyone was so used to for so many years did not stop because of the muddy streets or the dead bodies of gunmen laying here and there with their throats cut from ear to ear. The yelling from Hessenger demanding to find out who had done it wasn't going to help for the Indian warrior Mary

Hagger had seen looking at her was long gone; at least that's what she thought.

Opening the doors of the general store once again became a dreadful chore to Mary Hagger, but it was something to keep her mind stable and not give up hope that something would come to bring a change in her life. Preparing breakfast for the young man in the wine cellar was something she looked forward to doing each day and as she filled the basket with food, something hidden was rolled up in deer skin. Unrolling it, she found a note; it was from Truette it said that he would return for her and for her to keep her hopes and dreams in her heart as well as in her mind. Slowly turning around, she sensed that someone or something was standing behind her. As she finally saw what or who it was, she could not make a sound for Mary Hagger knew this Indian warrior had been sent by the cowboy. Motioning him to move into the backroom, Mary Hagger pulled her bed away from the wall to open a trap door on the wood floor. Down below a lantern lit up the room the size of the general store. Inside was food, water and guns. The Indian warrior who looked about twenty was surprised to see all the town's children. Three women stood beyond the children looking at the Indian warrior. One of them stepped up to him speaking in his language as she moved her hands in the air describing what she was saying.

The youngest was twelve but none of them was older than fifteen or sixteen years old. The woman was telling the Indian warrior that everyone had been living in that room for over twelve years since the evil old man and his men rode into Oakwood.

There was more than met the eye in Oakwood. The reason Mary Hagger had never told The Cowboy Bill Truette was because she had to make sure whose side he was on for Hessenger was very shrewd.

When the Cowboy had helped the young girl Sue and her daughter Betsy escape, Mary Hagger knew Truette was OK, but he was no longer there, only in her mind day in and day out... After Truette had gotten away with Sue and little Betsy, the telegram had been sent for help which the Cowboy could only pray would get there.

The loud knocks on the bedroom door told her it was not a customer, for they were more like a demand to be opened. Climbing out of the room beneath the store, she closed the trap door and moved her bed back on top of it made her buy a little time as she spoke that she was getting dressed. But she noticed a few muddy moccasin foot prints where the Indian warrior had first come into her room. Throwing some clothes over the footprints, she opened the door asking, "what's wrong, can't you all wait until I get out there - besides, you all never pay for anything anyway." Pushing her aside, one gunman looked under her bed and another in her closet as the third one asked her if she'd seen or heard anything out of the ordinary last night. Saying that the thunder was very loud, all three gunmen took a good look at her and told her she was lucky because Hessenger had said not to mess with her while they kept staring at her body until she pushed them out and closed the door. Standing with her back to the door, she trembled in fear and began to cry praying once more for help...

Meals had to be cooked at the same time for the children down below as for Harold Datson Jr. So no one could smell the food cooking down there. So many years had come and gone without anybody knowing about the children below.

The reason to put them in a safe place was, because Hessenger had ridden into Oakwood. Harold Datson Jr. was a boy of ten years of age. No one spoke of the children because Hessenger was said that he didn't like them and would kill them on the spot.

The sun began to dance its way down once again, which meant more danger loomed in the corners of the pitch night's moments. Releasing the Indian warrior had to be done at night. Mary Hagger had to tell the woman who spoke the native language, to please give Truette a note in returning to the Indian camp. Once again the Indian warrior had spoken before leaving and promised the woman he would return with more help.

Shots were fired into the night as Mary Hagger thought the Indian warrior had been caught, but the next day's evidence of more men found dead told her that he had gotten out of Oakwood safely. Speaking to the young man in the wine cellar would always ease Mary

Hagger's heart a little as she unrolled the biscuits and meat. She would also try to bring fresh carrots since she heard they would help vision. She began speaking of the messenger who had come in the the night to leave a note from the Cowboy that told of how he would come once more to help her out and clean Oakwood of the evil old man and his gunmen. For the first time she caught the attention of Harold Datson Jr. because he stood up and walked to a corner and spoke to her saying, "I had a dream last night kind of something like that, but the messenger had brought me some real guns with bullets in them. But it was just a dream like yours. He hadn't believed her story of the Indian warrior or the message she claimed to have received.

Taking all the food out of the basket, she told the young man that ever since he was a boy, she had tried to be like a mother, as she stood up once again as many times before and hugged him as she told him, I'll be back. Walking away a few steps, she spoke to him softly with her back to him, saying what would you do if I brought you a few loaded guns? The young man's response was to kill as many men as he could. Then she turned to look into his direction and said is that the only way you'll speak with me? You might kill a few men, maybe more. Then you'll get shot to death and that will be because of my careless mistake. When you can come up with a better plan than that, I'll bring you all the guns you want. Leaving, she spoke again, saying, I don't know why, but I feel like there's a reason you're still alive. He began to speak in a low voice saying that his father was once a gunman himself, but for the right side of the law. Then he sat down to eat as Mary Hagger walked up the steps and unlocked the door to let herself out. The sound of the door being locked once more made the young man hang his head as he began praying as tears flowed for now he understood that maybe one or two guns could help him kill a lot of gunmen, but once the guns were empty, they would kill him no matter who he was.

CHAPTER 12

Smoke from the PG ranch's chimney revealed life was normal in the midst of the meadows as the plan to bring down Hessenger in Oakwood took place. And the old miner had been chosen to do it alone. To draw out the evil old man would be a pleasure and to see to it that he would be stopped would ease the old miner's heart. Hessenger would have to die a very slow and painful death, which was the plan of the Indian Chief and his people.

On his donkey, the old miner Harold Datson Sr. would ride into Oakwood with a piece of gold the size of an eye wrapped in his handkerchief. But showing his hands would give away who he was and gloves had to be worn to hide the cut off fingers. A spot between two hills was chosen to be the area that Hessenger in town had to be taken as if more gold would be there.

The old miner ate breakfast with the Cowboy Bill Truette and the young woman Sue. He felt good as the Indian brave Bobby sat on the floor with little Betsy. The baby wolf Ring of Smoke sat next to little Betsy's rag doll ready to eat. Sue had never learned to cook, but the Cowboy would teach her and the usual chores around the ranch. Loading up the donkey, the old miner said his good byes and promised to bring back Hessenger and a bunch of his men.

Stepping along the side of the porch, the Cowboy told the old miner to be careful and that he would be waiting for him and the evil old man at the spot they had chosen. Sipping on the whiskey bottle to calm his nerves, Harold Datson Sr. rode his donkey slowly past some Indian warriors who had been his friends since the young braves had been little boys and in the years of knowing them, the old miner had showed them a thing or two. But his return would not be guaranteed and everyone's eyes told the old miner they knew what he was about to go do. For a long time the Indian Chief had told them all of the plans to end the killings in the town of Oakwood. Now the plan was in motion and no one was going to back down until the town was cleaned out.

Nodding to the braves, the old miner took another swig to ease his mind. Then another as he smiled and rode off alone. At times the donkey knew where to take the old miner as it headed for the trails which led the way into the direction of Oakwood.

It would take a while on the donkey's back and Truette needed all the time he could get so the help he had sent for might have enough time to arrive. Once the old miner got into Oakwood, he had to tell Hessenger about some more gold, but as he rode on many thoughts ran in his mind over and over again. Miles away from the PG ranch, he was away from everyone and alone where no one could see or hear him as he began to cry and speak out loud that someday he would like to see his son again. If he could still hold a gun like he used to, he would put holes into the evil old man and his gunmen for what they had done to him many years ago.

As the whiskey took effect on the old miner, he fell asleep on top of the donkey as they ambled on and on right into the middle of Oakwood. Looking at the old miner, the gunmen looked at each other smiling because he seemed harmless and broke as hell. Standing next to the stable, the donkey stood because of the strong smell of hay, the old miner started to wake up sliding on to the ground as the donkey went in for a bite to eat. On her way to feed the young man in the wine cellar, Mary Hagger dropped the basket of food and helped the old miner into the stable to get him out of harm's way. Harold Datson Sr. had one sip too many and was laid out cold on the ground. His gloves slipped off while Mary dragged him, revealing that his hands had both trigger fingers cut off. Putting the gloves back on and grabbing the bedroll, she covered him up. Leaving the stable, two gunmen passed by ordering her to mind her own business or else. Heading to the wine cellar to feed the young man.

She told Harold Datson Jr. about the old miner who had just ridden his donkey into Oakwood too drunk to stay on top. She also shared how she'd helped him into the stable and the oddest thing she'd ever seen was that the old miner's trigger fingers were cut off as his gloves had slipped off when she helped get him in the stable. She said she put them back on covering him up with the bedroll and how the gunmen told her to move on or else.

For the first time in all the years of knowing Mary Hagger, Harold Datson Jr. was now looking her straight in the eyes as he told her it had to be his father. He said that it had to be. With tears in his eyes and his voice trembling, he spoke of how many years ago Hessenger and his gunmen had come calling in the middle of the night asking Harold Datson Sr., his father, to work for him because he was also good with guns. But since his father refused to work for the evil old man, later that night the doors were kicked open and his father was beaten almost to death and his trigger fingers on each hand had been cut off so he would not be able to use guns any more. Harold Datson Jr. cried as he spoke of how he was forced to watch his father being tortured, then he was taken prisoner.

Revealing his secret of why he had been in that wine cellar all those years made Mary Hagger hugged him and assure him that she would do everything in her power to help in any way. She let him know she would be back with his next meal to let him know how his father was. As she began to leave, Harold Datson Jr. told her to tell his father how much he loved him and that he was still alive.

As Mary stepped out of the wine cellar and locked the door. A feeling of fear swept over her as she turned around seeing the old miner Harold Datson Sr. being dragged onto the hotel's wooden floor. Looking through the hotel windows, she saw the four gunmen dragging him in and begin to kick and beat the old miner until he spit up food from his mouth. Down on one knee, the old miner held himself up with one hand as he pulled out a handkerchief from his pocket and tossed it to the evil old man. Laughing he said that a few coins couldn't stop or wouldn't stop a beating for riding into Oakwood like he did. Then Hessenger's eyes widened up as he unrolled the handkerchief and saw the eye piece of gold. Ordering his men to stop beating the old miner, Hessenger told the old miner where in the hell did he get the gold from. Spitting more blood from his mouth as he wiped his lips, the old miner told Hessenger he would tell him where more gold was if he would promise to take care of him in Oakwood. The smile Hessenger gave the old miner could very well be seen that a lie was to follow but the bait was set. The greed for money and gold would blind any fool.

The old miner asked to speak with him alone and Hessenger agreed saying sure, anything for a friend. As he told the old miner to follow him upstairs to his room, the young pretty girl who was chosen to take Sue's place was pushed outside. But not one gunman dared to laugh because of how he had shot one of them between the eyes for laughing at him before. Outside the hotel windows, Mary looked on but was told to move along as gunmen walked past her. From the windows of the general store she kept watching to see what was going on and in a few minutes the evil old man and about ten gunmen saddled up horses and rode out of town. The same buggy Sue and little Betsy used for their picnic ride hauled the old miner and would carry more gold as the bait had worked. But Mary had no clue what was going on, only what she had seen. During the next meal, she told the young man in the wine cellar all that had happened as she began to pray out loud for Harold Datson Jr.

The noon sun beamed down on the gunmen as they rode out of town in search for more gold as the old miner had promised was waiting to be dug up. The sneer of greed the evil old man was wearing could be seen a mile away. Out in front of the buggy rode four gunmen, one drove the buggy and Hessenger sat next to the driver. Behind them in the distance four more gunmen came along. With his back to the buggy, the old miner sat up looking at the four riders behind them and even though it had been twelve years ago, Harold Datson Sr. could still see each one who held him down while the evil old man had cut off his fingers, before riding off with his son. The only thing that kept them from knowing who he was. Was the long scraggly hair and the salt and pepper beard that held his face and the old leather gloves that hid his cut off fingers.

Sparking up a conversation, the old miner asked Hessenger if he'd brought a bottle of whiskey. Over his shoulder he handed over a bottle of whiskey and told him to make it last. Nervousness overpowered the old miner as he took big quips of pure whiskey like it was water. A few miles down the trail, he started to speak with the four riders as they smiled at him because soon they thought they would be rich instead of dead. The four riders at the rear were much older than the ones he'd seen up front. For he hoped that the young riders would not see the ambush up ahead.

When Hessenger finds the gold, he had plans of his own. To do away with the younger gunmen for they could not be trusted with the location of the gold. The gunman who sat next to Hessenger asked if he liked the four younger gunmen up front. Laughter broke the thoughts of Harold Datson Sr. as he was now getting a good feeling from the whiskey bottle. Hessenger told the buggy driver, "you're my right hand man and whatever you say goes along way with me." Well, that's good to know, remarked the buggy driver with a big grin on his face he told the evil old man that once the gold was found, he would shoot each one and keep their share. He also said that he would make sure the evil old man made it back to town safe. They both looked at each other and laughed out loud as Hessenger smiled and said, I knew there was a reason I got you to be my right hand man. With a serious face, Hessenger told the buggy driver that he had learned too many tricks, but he'd learned to play his cards very well.

Stopping for a night's rest each rider stretched and began to make a camp fire for the night. Harold Datson Sr. was tied to the wheel of the buggy and told if he tried to escape, his fingers on both hands would be cut off. Looking straight into Hessenger's eyes, the old miner know that he was serious about what he said because it was his trademark. Then another gunman who stood next to the buggy driver told him he'll just throw him in the wine cellar with the kid...That really made Harold Datson Sr. real mad because now he actually didn't know if it had been a joke or if they really knew who he was and had been playing along all the time.

Thinking that if at the time many years ago he would had agreed to Hessenger's offers to hire his guns. That maybe his son would never be where he was or if he still lived. The tears began to roll out of the old miner's eyes as Hessenger stood over him saying that he promised not to hurt him if he took him straight to the gold. But Harold Datson Sr. once again in the embrace of Hessenger knew to outwit this type of man. He could not trust him to hold his word to anything or anyone.

The moonlight shined a gentle glow over the land as the sound of wolves howling into the night took place. Studying the gunmen, they all laid out cold and slept like babies as Hessenger laid on the ground next to the buggy driver, his eyes not yet a- sleep, stared at Harold Datson Sr. as he spoke softly to him saying if he had ever met him somewhere. The old miner looked at him and began to roll to the other side as he stated that if he'd met him somewhere, he'd already be rich and owned a place in Oakwood. Rolling around had ended the conservation, but not the pain of the ropes which had been used to tie his hands to the buggy wheel.

The sparkling stars and the dark peaceful night with a gentle glow from the moon seemed like the only true home Harold Datson Sr. had had in so very long. But the thought of how peaceful the PG ranch had been brought a smile to the old miner's face as Ring of Smoke, the baby wolf danced in his mind.

Untying his hands from the buggy wheel awoke Harold Datson Sr. as it had seemed the night was just a little too short, but a sip from the whiskey bottle would cure all that. Grabbing a bite to eat didn't take long either as Hessenger barked out orders to get ready to ride out. No one spoke for hours, then Hessenger asked the old miner how far is this place and how much you reckon is there. The old miner asked to stop the buggy and let him stand up to see where they were. Pointing in the direction of rolling hills, the old miner stated that between those two over to the left was the spot. A big smile took over the emotions the evil man had and ordered to ride the buggy faster but be careful.

Pulling his gun from his holster, Hessenger checked to see if it was loaded and placed it back into the holster. The area was close now and Harold Datson Sr. told the evil old man to stop the buggy. As the buggy rolled to a stop, the gunmen got off their horses and tied them to the buggy. Walking a while as he looked at the ground, Harold Datson Sr. was giving Truette enough time to see them. Looking at one hill and then the other, the old miner stood up and stomped on the ground to let the evil old man know it was the spot. Hessenger and his gunmen all smiled as each began to get some shovels from the back of the buggy. The old miner sat on the ground next to the buggy in case the shooting started.

Digging a hole knee high, the evil old man told everyone to stop the digging and looked at Harold Datson Sr. with a puzzled look. But the Old miner looked back at him and said just a little deeper and you're the richest man alive. The digging started back up when one of the youngest gunmen hit a rock and hit it again. The third time, he brought up a piece of gold the size of a man's fist. Silence took its place as everyone stood looking at the gold. Then Hessenger's eyes turned to look at his right hand man.

As fast as lightning, he shot one after the other until all four young gunmen were dead. He said in a low dry voice, them boys still too wet behind the ears for this land. The laughter was from greed, not the happiness of how the evil old man felt as they pulled the dead young gunmen from the hole. Sure liked to bury them, but it's not like me to do these boys that favor, besides we got to feed the buzzes something. Then the laughter started again as they dug up another big chunk of gold.

The old miner now knew the Indian Chief's plan was and had worked for now. Not only was Hessenger showing his true colors, but there was four less gunmen to kill and by now the eyes of The Cowboy Bill Truette and many warriors were keeping an eye out. In moments it would be over.

Hessenger then told the other gunmen to cover up the hole up quickly and ride out because something didn't feel right. Two gold nuggets in the middle of nowhere, he said just didn't add up. We'll be back later to dig up the rest. Looking at the old miner while talking to him saying that if anything happens, you're the first to die. Leaving very fast as the buggy rode on, Harold Datson Sr. wondered what had just taken place. Where were the Cowboy and the Indian warriors? The gold had seemed too easy to find and Hessenger had figured something was not right. Riding all day faster than they had come had caused them to pass the place they had camped out the night before.

As the sun set for another night out in the open, Hessenger stated, no camp fire tonight boys and as soon as we can, we're out of here in the morning. Wondering if the Cowboy had heard the shots when the four young gunmen had been killed in cold blood out in the open, it made the old miner ponder even more and now knew for a fact no one had heard any shots.

Hessenger smiled at Harold Datson Sr. and told him, I have a special place for you since you like to drink so much and you'd better pray more gold is there the next time we go back.

The right hand manstood next to Harold Datson Sr. Looking at him with a puzzled face and told him, I'd bet my bottom dollar we've met somewhere before, but I just can't put my finger on it right now.

Rolling out bed rolls and using saddles for pillows made the night a little comfortable. As Hessenger held the gold nugget in front of him, he smiled at the old miner and said, I felt something back there, like I feel about you, old miner, right now so why don't you make it easy for both of us and tell me where have we met. Looking at the stars, the old miner needed answers himself but one answer he had needed to know was what had happened to his son, Harold Datson Jr. Then anger arose within him that he put into his mind to escape and it had to be that night because once back in Oakwood it would be very hard to get out alive with so many gunmen he'd seen with his own eyes. In the view of some gunmen, it had seemed that it was a must to work for Hessenger. He could see the fear in their eyes. As Hessenger had made it very, very clear – you work for him or die.

Slowly one by one, the gunmen started to fall asleep and as the old miner tried to loosen the ropes from behind his back. The only one not asleep was the night watchman. Hessenger had chosen his right hand man to take the first watch. For Hessenger trusted him with his life. He never went anywhere without him. He was like a shadow that followed him everywhere. But now, Hessenger laid sound asleep as the right hand man kept moving around on the lookout for anything out of the ordinary night's way.

CHAPTER 13

Mounting his horse, Truette looked into the eyes of Sue and her little girl Betsy, promising each one that Hessenger in Oakwood would never come back into their lives again and that he would return shortly.

As Sue handed her uncle his rifle, the Cowboy placed it in its saddle scabbard and nodded to the many Indian braves the Indian Chief had sent to watch the PG ranch while the Cowboy was away. Yet along side the trails as he rode away, many, many more joined in behind him. None could speak English, but safety would be for sure with him. In the direction of the mountains he went to wait for Hessenger and a handful of his men. His return was not certain, but it had to be done to put an end to Hessenger's wild rampage of killing and doing as he pleased. Looking at the braves who held a look in their faces of an unknown hunt, yet each one knew his life was put on the line. Bill Truette rode his horse ahead of all the braves and none could have his sparkling eyes as tears formed from thinking of his own family. Also needing to know if his boss had received the telegram or if he even was still alive to help because bringing down Hessenger might be easy, but it wouldn't be to bring down the gunmen in Oakwood.

Through the mountains and valleys away from Devil's Din Desert that ran across North Clayton was where the old miner was to bring Hessenger. Once there the Cowboy and Indian braves ambush the greedy evil old man and his gunmen were digging for gold. But no shooting would be made until the old miner was well out of the way. As Truette looked at each Indian brave and what they were to shoot with would only be arrows, because he was the only one with a gun and rifle. But the smoothness of death was held in many ways, especially from the young Indians who held a magic in the way each could use the bow and arrows on horseback at full speed or under the horse's belly as they hid their bodies from harm's way on the horses. Running or walking, sitting and even crawling, they all could kill with arrows. At times if the arrow only cut the skin, death would eventually make its call as poisons were mixed and soaked into the arrowheads. Most Indian braves would shoot arrows at the same time high and low and one or many more would hit the body of the enemy. At night, the Indians were more deadly, but this time it had to be daylight because the Cowboy had his guns and Hessenger with his gunmen would be too busy digging for gold. Not a sound would be made until death was upon its calling and it loomed in the night's moonlight but had to wait till full daylight because nothing would be left standing, only Hessenger alone or at least that was the plan the Cowboy had been told from the Indian Chief.

The reason to bring Hessenger in alive was to try and make him tell all his gunmen in Oakwood to surrender, which was a one in a million chance. Even to save his own life. But once caught, Hessenger would be punished very slowly next to the river's running waters as the spirits would be called to collect his soul. The Cowboy knew if it ever came time that someone would or could get a chance to overpower Hessenger, it meant death then and there for anyone who would wear those boots. The evil old man would kill anyone on the spot.

Arriving at the place where Hessenger might make camp for the night, the Cowboy started to make plans on how to ambush the gunmen in the morning. The Cowboy hid behind some rocks on the hills above the place where a few gold nuggets had been buried as bait days ago, As the dawn's light shined down, the Indian warriors sent out howls in the air to one another to find out how far they sat apart. As Truette had taken a higher spot for his rifle's range to hit its targets at any area around.

The brim of Truette's hat hid the morning's blazing sun from his face as the Cowboy began to daydream of everything that had happened to him. Where life had brought him now seeking to undo what an evil old man had created, but he could not fail or his new family might not make it. Over the edges of the rocks he could see the young Indian warriors placing their lives on the line for him, a white man. But the real reason was to honor their Chief's wishes to help bring down Hessenger and his hired gunmen once and for all.

Harold Datson Sr. for sure wanted Hessenger in his sights when the fight started. Datson had once told the Cowboy that the Indian Chief had been the only one to know his past. But to the Cowboy, it really did not matter, because the old miner now had made a friend no matter what. Focusing on ideas of how to bring down the hired gunmen in Oakwood was harder than the Cowboy could see and once again wonder if the telegram had made it out. If so and the outfit's boss was still there at the Silver Star, which brand held the double S symbol, the Cowboy knew in his heart help would arrive. But since it had been ten years, chances were slim because the Indian warriors wouldn't have a chance against the gunmen with rifles in Oakwood. unless there was an ambush, like the one planned for that day.

Another howl and whistle told the cowboy to stay alert and not wander off into another daydream. As he could see a warrior point into the distance sky at an eagle that was flying by, as if it was their eyes to see in the distance.

Truette had seen many men die, but not like the killing Hessenger the situation in Oakwood had gotten out of control. And it seemed that everything in the town belonged to Hessenger, the evil old man without a care for human life. Thinking about the little girl three years of age, Betsy Randalls Hessenger, whose father had married Sue Randalls, now Sue Randalls Hessenger under Hessenger's own laws in Oakwood, made the Cowboy want to kill him even more. Raising the little girl would be the easy part, but telling her he'd had to kill her father would be no easy task at all. But death could be the only way Hessenger could or would be stopped.

The morning sun beamed over the hills as four gunmen lay dead and the shadow of what was thought to be an eagle turned out to be a buzzard.

Hessenger had been there already and gone. Just as before, more men were left for dead, a trademark of his evil acts was done once more, even on his own men. His greed for wealth and power seems to consume him more and more each day.

As the Cowboy began using his ability to track down and read traces of movement. Truette could tell what had happened, seeing the four gunmen dead was another thing, knowing how long they had left told him a day before because of the dug up dirt and that the greed of what was found made Hessenger kill his own men. The gold had been found and where the buggy wheels had stopped once was three or four spits from a human who badly hurt and he knew it had to be the old miner beat up, but how bad, that he would not be able to tell. But Harold Datson Sr. was still alive. As the Cowboy mounted his horse and started to ride at a high gallop for it was a must to catch up to the buggy before it reached Oakwood.

The Indian warriors rode right along beside him as they had figured it out, too. Almost noon and it was time the horses needed a rest or they would ride them to their death. They sat opposite of their horses on the ground for shade, but Truette stood true and ready, looking on far into the distance for any traces coming or going. The brim of his hat hid the sun from his face as he drifted back into another daydream of how life had dealt his hand and to win he knew he would have to focus as he snapped back into reality taking the gun out of his holster making sure it was loaded and ready to use. It was easy to tell what time it was as he stuck a stick in the ground that showed a nub of shadow at the bottom left side of the stick. This told him it was almost one in the afternoon. Sitting in the open land had brought him a moment of silence as he looked at the Indian warriors, but he could not speak to them. But in his mind, he knew they could count on him to kill Hessenger or any of the hired gunmen in or out of Oakwood.

Memories of Mary Hagger's sweet smell and gentle body when he had only touched once danced in the Cowboy's mind, then the last word his wife told him before he had to shoot her. "Infinity" was what she'd said that had been a love she always wanted him to know she had for him.

Voices of his boss at the Silver Stars outfit also rang in his mind as the old man, his boss, told him to send for help any time he needed it. Ten years later, sitting in a land out in the open with Indian warriors as friends would be hard for anyone to believe because his job was once avoiding being seen by his enemies, the red skins.

Thinking about how the Chief had raised Bobby the young white warrior as his own son made the Cowboy realize the Indians had a good heart since they were risking their lives to bring down Hessenger. In Truette's mind, he could remember telling the old miner to give the Indian warrior who was the messenger a note to Mary Hagger. If she had gotten it or not, even if the messenger was skillful enough to make it out in or out of Oakwood. Many thoughts touched the four corners of his mind but one thought never left - that he would survive to see Mary Hagger again. For some strange reason, she had captured his heart or maybe the Cowboy was just lonely in life once again.

Looking down at the ground, Truette was deep into his thoughts of when he'd first seen Devil's Din Desert and Crystal Pit Canyon; so beautiful during the day, but much more dangerous at night. It held a special place in his heart for he had ridden through these places with his wife Amy, but the unforgettable moment was when he had delivered his baby girl, Patty Ann.

As he relived those times, he lingered on the thought of where he might be buried if he died this moment. Then the PG grave appeared in his mind and how it all started replayed again as he rode up on the PG ranch.

Many men had died in his life trying him, but only three had never done anything to him, but he had killed them anyway. He'd slit the buggy driver's throat from ear to ear the day he helped Sue and her little Betsy escape, plus the two gunmen he killed later that day at the picnic area. The shrieks of bullets piercing the backs of the gunmen still flashed in his mind. Luck was on his side that day and seemed to still be on his side right now for he still lived for the chance to help kill Hessenger, who was miles away and almost in Oakwood as he would once again hide behind his own men.

Hours passed and the sun showed to be at least four in the afternoon. A good rest for the horses and for the Cowboy. The tracks of the buggy could be followed as once in a while drops of dry blood to the side of the trail of wheels would appear. His friend Harold Datson Sr. who the Cowboy only knew as the old miner was hurt and out of whiskey because an empty bottle laid on the old dusty trail.

The Cowboy gave a moment's touch of his little wolf, Ring of Smoke, as he smiled remembering each time he blew a ring of smoke from his cigarette, the baby wolf would howl. In the loneliest time in his life after he lost his family, he'd made a friend in a cold blizzard storm in an old abandoned stable. Touching his face, he could feel the scar on his cheek where Hessenger had planted one of his spurs the day he'd got beaten up in the wooden floor of the hotel. Hessenger had gotten away with too much and had to be put to a stop. But the Indian Chief wanted him alive to punish him dearly. As the Indian people were masters of punishing an enemy to make him talk, then make him wish he'd not made a sound. That was all good to the Cowboy and to watch would be a pleasure, but at the moment, it seemed Hessenger had gotten away, outsmarting everyone for he was nowhere in sight. Resting a few more hours before the Cowboy and Indian warriors rode out again meant it would be the last time for a stop since Hessenger and his few men had to be caught before reaching Oakwood. Remembering that the Indians had never gotten into a white man's war reminded him of how many times as a scout he'd avoided coming close to the red man's camps and guided army trails to the mountains away from trouble. Oakwood now stood where those trails were for the oak wood tree was a mark on a map that didn't show towns. But now not long after a town was built, Hessenger and his hired gunmen took over and no one could leave once there. Over twelve years Oakwood rested not one night in fear as death to anyone who didn't obey the evil old man's wishes had held everyone from bonding as one or even think to try and go against the laws of Hessenger had put in place when he took over.

From what the old miner told the Cowboy translating for the Indian Chief, the army had not been seen much and had gone farther away from Oakwood once the white man's war was over. Settlers had come to build the small town now called Oakwood, which Hessenger stole with fear he'd instilled upon the people.

The Cowboy now found himself the guide to put an end to the evil acts that took place in the small town out in the empty openness that only the Indian people and Hessenger's captives had come to know. The thought of the message he'd sent Mary Hagger lingered in his mind.

As the sun's beaming heat sent shimmering waves across the horizon, far in the distance a trail of dust sent a message to Truette that more than one rider was up ahead and coming his way. In a short while as the sun made its move, the Cowboy could clearly see a buggy high-tailing it toward them. All thoughts came to an end as the Cowboy pointed to let the Indian warriors know the buggy was on its way. Surrounding the buggy, the Cowboy could not believe his eyes.

CHAPTER 14

The howling of wolves echoed through the valley as it had every night before as thunderous lightning sent flashes of light through Oakwood. The Indian messenger had crawled on his belly into town and cut six gunmen's throats. He then gave Mary Hagger the message from the Cowboy in the deerskin and she hid him in the room under the general store for the night. Scouring the town inch by inch, the hired gunmen had asked her if she'd seen anything. Risking her life was a normal but extremely dangerous feat she had mastered in Oakwood or die. The following night, the Indian messenger left as he had a message to get back to the Cowboy from Mary Hagger. Leaving in the same manner he arrived, the Indian messenger slit seven more throats of gunmen which made a night's watch easy to do. Killing six one night and seven the next, Oakwood was in a state of shock, but it was too late. The Indian messenger was crawling in the direction of a dark camp he'd noticed some time ago. The exact spot where Earl Hessenger slept used to be the young Indian's old stomping grounds.

The glistening moonlight glowed upon the vast plain as the right hand man took watch for the night. Drinking cold black coffee because Hessenger had said no camp fire for the night in fear of being spotted. The horses were tied on one side of the buggy and Harold Datson Sr.

on the other. Creeping past the horses that were in a trance as their big eyes knew not to draw attention to themselves. Because even an animal could tell death was near and avoided to invite it close by.

In a very low whisper the Indian messenger spoke to the old miner as he cut the ropes that bound him to the buggy. The right hand man stood tall as he was to take first watch as he stood looking at the sparkling stars. Hessenger and the other four gunmen slept peacefully until the tin cup hit a rock when the watchman dropped it as his throat had been sliced from ear to ear. Flipping in the air once, then twice between two gunmen, the Indian messenger slit each one's throat. The other two gunmen and Hessenger lay yards away and the Indian messenger would not get there in time, as they rose up from a dead sleep trying to focus on what was going on. The peals of loud rifle shots rang out into the night as the last two gunmen dropped to the ground. Harold Datson Sr. could still use a rifle, but not a gun. Then he shouted to Hessenger walking towards him as he told him to try his luck and draw his guns. Quickly Hessenger threw his hands up into the dark sky as he begged for mercy pleading with the old miner not to shoot. Harold Datson Sr. laid him out cold with the butt of the rifle. Bending down to where Hessenger had been sleeping, he picked up the whiskey bottle.

Tying Hessenger up and tossing him atop the buggy, the Indian messenger pulled a burlap sack from under the seat and placed it over

Hessenger's head. Riding into the dark trails leading back towards the hills, the Indian messenger spoke to the old miner, Harold Datson Sr. as he handed him the message Mary Hagger wanted the Cowboy to have.

The gunmen's horses would walk to town alone as the other gunmen in Oakwood would try to figure out what had happened. Next to each other the Indian messenger and Harold Datson Sr. laughed out loud, even though they were not safe yet. The Indian messenger was skilled at bringing death quickly and leaving as soon as the message was given. And this one went very well as he'd killed sixteen gunmen by himself to the two the old miner had for his count. At least after his fingers had been cut off many years ago. Harold Datson Sr. back in his days on the right side of the law was called when dangerous gunmen rolled into towns trying to make names for themselves. Falling in love had caused Harold Datson Sr. to put an end to his carrying guns. As the years went by, he moved on, ending up close to Devil's Din Desert and Crystal Pit Canyon. Building a small ranch and a stable, while his wife had a baby boy he'd named Harold Datson Jr. after his wife died in childbirth. Never being the same, he tried to give his son a good life by hiding away his guns. Years later Hessenger rode into his life wanting him to work as a hired gunman. Refusing had caused the evil old man to turn Harold Datson Sr. and his son's lives upside down as his fingers had been cut off and his son was taken away.

Hessenger was now his prisoner and he could easily kill him, but the Indian Chief's friendship had brought killing new meaning. Hessenger would die, yet it would be a very painful death. The kind that would take days to claim a body and the soul to be taken away as the Indian people's ways were thought that spirits could still punish a soul forever. Besides there were more folks who would like to see Hessenger die and witnessing his death was like a basic need that had to be filled.

So he had to bring Hessenger back alive only to die as planned by the Indian Chief.

If it had not been for the Indian messenger, Hessenger would have gotten away and continued to overpower everyone or anyone who crossed his path. Helpless he now sat all tied up and out cold in the back of the buggy.

Without a leader, Oakwood would become a graveyard sooner than it would be if Hessenger was still there, for the gunmen needed to be told when and when not to kill or they would always kill as it ran in their blood. Mary would not be safe anymore and Harold Datson Jr. would die first.

The gunmen would use all the men in Oakwood as targets while the women would be used more than they were already being used for wild nights out on the town. Spitting more blood from his mouth, the old miner looked back into the buggy. As they rode on an anger stole his thoughts as he hit the evil old man once more with the butt of his rifle. The rabbit skin had been stuffed safely in his" boot that held the note from Mary to the Cowboy. Bill Truette was her only hope of making it and the only hope of saving the children under the general store who'd hidden there for twelve years.

Pointing into the darkened sky, the Indian messenger spoke to the old miner. As he saw the falling star, he made a wish as he had many nights before to someday see his son again. Then a sparkle Slid down his face as a tear disappeared into his beard.

He took a sip of whiskey, and then another. As the night slipped away, many more miles stood behind them and Oakwood was even further which meant it was safer as the moments passed. But only safer for Harold Datson Sr. and the Indian messenger. For the folks of Oakwood when the sun came out and Hessenger no longer barked out orders as he'd done for twelve years. Life would change from one day to the next as each gunman would try and rule each other until one would become the boss. Hessenger had been gone for two nights and Oakwood was in the midst of falling apart as each gunman passed each other it seemed that each one had a need in their mind to see who could be faster with their guns. Women, wine, whiskey and beer were the only true friends the gunmen really knew, besides their one and only - the gun in their holsters. As patience was running thin in

Oakwood, the lives of everyone were at risk on the streets day or night.

The Indian Messenger told Harold Datson Sr. of the children in the room under the general store. Bringing the buggy to a full stop, the old miner looked at his new friend and asked him if a blonde kid about twenty two was there. Thinking for a while, the Indian messenger shook his head. He hadn't seen anyone like that. Dropping his head, the old miner slapped the reins on the horses back to motion the buggy to carry on. He then went off into deep thoughts of killing the evil old man at that point.

The dawn's light gently came into focus as the miles behind them slipped away, yet somehow Oakwood would need as much help to rise up again into the town it once was. In Harold Datson Sr.'s mind, He knew he would have to return once more as the blood from his mouth became thicker each time. He was hurt from the gunmen's beating when he first arrived in Oakwood on his donkey.

The blazing sun at the back of the buggy aimed its burning flames as sweat rolled down Harold Datson Sr.'s and the Indian messenger's body. But it was not as bad as it was for the evil old man who wore the burlap sack over his head and shoulders.

As the dust flew past them from the back for the wind had made a turn, the same direction they rode.

The buggy moved fast into the rolling hills, but not as fast for the old miner who wished he'd already returned to the Indian camp. There he'd find the two bottle of whiskey in the cold river that would taste so good to him.

Up ahead the old miner could see trail of dust blowing away from him, but he knew the riders were coming his direction as the wind was still at his back. A big smile overtook his emotions as he elbowed the sleeping Indian messenger next to him. He knew that it had to be the Cowboy Bill Truette and his young Indian warriors.

Removing his old worn out dusty hat, the old miner waved it in the-air and saw the Cowboy up ahead doing the same. Coming to a stop, the Cowboy listened to the old miner's story of the children living under the general store. Then he grabbed the rabbit skin with the note wrapped inside from Mary Hagger. Taking a deep breath Truette wished he could ride into Oakwood with a handful of Indian warriors, but he knew he'd die before he could make it in.

Hoping help would arrive from the Silver Star ranch where his boss may have already rode out to come to help if the message had gotten to him or if he was still alive. Waiting for help would happen at the PG ranch, but if no one showed up, their plans would have to change.

As the Cowboy and his friends came into sight, Sue, Bobby, and little Betsy ran to the entrance of the PG corral to greet them. On the porch the little wolf Ring of Smoke stood like the king of a mountain as he howled his little heart out. For Truette his master was home once again. Getting off the buggy, the old miner fell off the side as the young Indian warriors ran to help him get up.

Truette could tell his friend was hurt as he spit thick blood, hurt badly and needed a medicine man as soon as he could get there.

The Cowboy told the old miner that it would be better to go into the Indian camp where Hessenger would not have a chance to get away and to get help for him, too. The PG ranch stood still as everyone had left to the Indian camp with Hessenger on the back of the buggy.

Arriving at the camp of the Indian Chief, Hessenger was taken away with all four limbs tied to trees, but the burlap sack was still over his head and shoulders.

The Indian Chief spoke to his people with his hands moving letting them know who the prisoner was tied to the trees. As the fire keeper prepared to light the fires that would glow over the Indian camp that signaled the coming of the night, this let every one who could see that the red man was ready for another torture of a soul who would be given to the spirits over the cold river's waters to take and punish for the rest of its life. Then and only then would people rest in knowing Hessenger was long gone, into an endless land of no return for he would slowly die. In the cruel hands of the Indians, who were masters of death; one that seemed to take forever.

Food and water lay with the tepees where Sue, Betsy and the Cowboy would spend the night. Truette needed some peace and quiet, but nothing like Sue and little Betsy who were moments away from a lifetime of torture at the hands of the soon dead evil old man Earl Hessenger, who was now harmless in the hands of his enemies. The white man's war which the Indian Chief and his people never fought for or against was now a must to kill so many could flee the embrace of Hessenger. But back in Oakwood, the hired gunmen would soon come to wonder what had happened and maybe come looking for their boss or just sit and wait as told before leaving.

Ring of Smoke's howls into the night sent chills into Hessenger's body as the little wolf stared into his eyes as the burlap sack was being removed, looking over the fire into the camp stood many warriors around Hessenger. As each eye told him that escape was out of the question. In the distance was Harold Datson Sr. sitting on the ground, sipping on the cold bottle of whiskey he'd found in the cold river. Not having to call him over the old miner stood up and headed towards Hessenger. As he glared into his eyes, the old miner told him tomorrow you will come to know who I am. But that others wanted to speak to him first. Spitting into Hessenger's face, he told him that he would soon regret every evil deed he ever did. Hessenger's face as he threatened in a low cut dry voice, that his hired gunmen could see to it that the old miner would die before his eyes.

Harold Datson Sr. spit once more on Hessenger's forehead slowly turning around saying it would be his last night alive and to make it last. Anger took over as Hessenger began to yell out orders as he'd barked them out for years to fools who had been bought from the devil himself. Then one of the Indian warriors knocked him out with a piece of bone from the jaws of a buffalo that lay next to the fire keeper.

A full moon filled the sky's empty vastness as it lit up the ground below. But the flames from the blazing fire danced even higher. As whispers to the spirits were being sent by the fire keeper that Hessenger would soon be theirs to keep. Sitting in front of Hessenger, an old Indian warrior beat the drums gently as he sang in his native Indian tongue. Two more Indian warriors stuck the handkerchief in his mouth that still held the gold nugget the size of an eye that was used to trick Hessenger out of Oakwood. The gold nugget meant nothing to the Indian people as it did and had for Hessenger for so many years. Now bound to the trees, he waited to be tortured the following day.

CHAPTER 15

Beyond the rolling hills towards Oakwood, a thin string of smoke led its way upward into the moonlit sky. Not only was the fire from the Indian camp burning in the midst of the night. As the Cactus Inn Saloon had been set on fire and no one was allowed to put out or try to put the fire. The hired gunmen with a gut feeling that their boss Earl Hessenger would never return began drinking and shooting up anything in sight. Screaming for their lives, the townspeople began to panic as they ran out to see the fire. Their lives ended abruptly with bullets piercing through their bodies from all directions. Dead bodies laid out in the street as Mary Hagger looked on from the windows of the general store.

After twelve years hoping and praying for help to come, it seemed that her fight for life would end. But not without a fight as she ran to her room and pulled the bed away from the trap door that led into the room beneath the general store. Handing everyone rifles as she grabbed one herself, she told the children and three women that hiding would no longer be safe because if her store was set on fire, they all would burn to death.

Out the back door, she led them into the pitch dark night.

The inferno from the Cactus Inn Saloon was entertaining the gunmen giving Mary Hagger time to lead them into safety. Oakwood would not be a safe place to be and out in open land it would be dangerous as well. For only little water and food had been taken with them.

More smoke billowed into the sky as Mary Hagger told everyone that another building had been set on fire and to please move on into the dark empty land. Dropping to her knees, she began to cry as one of the older children came to her side asking her what was wrong. She stood up and said that she had to go back or the young man in the wine cellar would die alone.

She told the three women to keep on going without her as she grabbed a sack of food along with five loaded pistols and two boxes of bullets. Back in the general store, she looked out the windows as two gunmen passed by. For so many years she had come and gone in and out of the hotel that she had to keep acting as if nothing was wrong as she'd only come to feed the young man.

Opening the wine cellar door, she quickly locked it behind her and began telling the young man Harold Datson Jr. that Oakwood had been set on fire and soon the hotel would be set ablaze as well. The sound of bullets were getting louder as more gunmen got drunk and shot up the town.

Harold Datson Jr. stood up and asked Mary Hagger why she had riskcd her life for him and that it didn't make any sense since she was too afraid to bring him a loaded gun anyway. Emptying the sack of food along with the five pistols with two boxes of bullets onto the floor made the young man's eyes glow like never before.

As Harold Datson Jr. bent over to pick up a gun, Mary told him to please kill for the good reasons in life. Dropping the first gun as he spun it in his hand, the gun fell perfectly into the holster as he told Mary Hagger that all the years she tried to teach him had not gone to wastc because he had been paying close attention to her all along. As he hugged her promising to do the right thing, he stuck another gun in the rope of his holster and the other in the back as he now held one in each hand ready to walk out of the wine cellar for the first time in his life. The words Mary Hagger spoke for many years rang in his mind of where each porch and building were from each other. But that didn't help knowing where the gunmen would be standing as each had his own mind to do as they pleased because Hessenger no longer was there.

As the door swung open from the wine cellar, Harold Datson Jr. stepped out with his guns in his hands, looking into the eyes of three gunmen. As he spoke to them in a low cut voice and told them the party was over. Before the gunmen could reach for their guns, He had taught himself very well how to use a gun because when he pulled the triggers, the bullets hit dead center into the gunmen's chests.

The three gunmen had died in moments as Harold Datson Jr. now stood outside the hotel entrance, but only two more gunmen noticed him as he stepped around the corner of the hotel following him and Mary Hagger. The voice could have been a bullet, but because the gunmen thought they were really fast that told Mary Hagger and Harold Datson Jr. to slowly put up their hands in the air.

Both hands in the air, he was ordered to turn around. Looking into the eyes of Harold Datson Jr., one gunman ordered him to drop his guns as they smiled at him. Dropping both guns from above his head, he caught them both midair next to his hips. The swarms of bullets echoed into the night sent the two gunmen down to the ground dead before they could blink an eye. Mary Hagger stood in shock as she had witnessed the young man kill five gunmen without even thinking. The lightning speed of how he'd moved his arms as his hands had perfectly caught the guns in midair was amazing, but doing it in pitch darkness was unbelievable. Not only was Harold Datson Jr. very fast with the guns, he had mastered his respect the instant touch of them for he now spoke in a voice Mary Hagger found strange, but respectful in its own way.

Stepping out into the dark night, Mary Hagger told the young man of the children and three women up ahead. After a few more steps, Harold Datson Jr. stood looking back at Oakwood. She spoke softly to him, telling him they could not go back.

The third building went up in smoke as the women and children took a break and rested. Mary Hagger and the young man caught up with them. After all those years of being alone in the wine cellar, he sat by himself far away from everyone. As he could hear Mary Hagger tell them how fast he'd been with his guns. He went off into his thoughts of how his father once told him someday I might show you how to use a gun. In his mind he had seen himself peeking into the stable as his father practiced with his guns. What he'd seen had never been erased from his mind, and now he possessed the talents in using guns for all the right reasons. Reloading them as he sat in thought, Mary handed him something to eat and drink, but the young man seemed not to notice her in front of him. Bending over in front of him, she saw that his eyes were closed as he loaded the guns as if he'd been looking right at them. In her mind he was good and she'd seen he was lightning fast as well, but in her heart she knew he, as a man with guns, would crave to kill once again.

Reaching out for the food and water as he'd placed the guns down, he never opened his eyes as he told Mary, I knew you'd been there a while. He also thanked her for she'd been the one to show him how to use his mind's eye. Then he opened his eyes as he said, the Cowboy who came to Oakwood would be a very lucky man for you. Then he spoke of how not to lose hope as faith was also to stay in her heart. She had thought of the young man more than she could ever imagine and now he was being loyal to her, for he would stay close by and keep her safe.

Harold Datson Jr. knew in his heart he would meet up with more gunmen, as the night grew into an endless wait to prove he was as good as his father was once with guns. He stood ready in the midst of the black night for at any minute the gunmen would come calling on him and Mary Hagger.

***

The howls of distant wolves went out into the vast barren land ready to claim a lost soul and if anyone strayed from the others it would mean a meal to them. Mary Hagger knew what the howls of wild wolves meant, as she told everyone to stay together and not panic and run. The moon shined its glow as four gunmen's silhouettes came into focus calling Mary Hagger to come forth.

Harold Datson Jr. spoke to them as he told them who he was. Also that it would be nice to try them in a fair gunfight, but would they do it was out of the question as bullets tore into the night awards Harold Datson Jr. and Mary Hagger. Then out of nowhere, the sounds of rifles rang out very loudly as all the children laid on the ground shooting back at the gunmen. The silhouettes no longer stood in the glow of the night, for each gunman had found what they'd been looking for and it was their deaths that came as a surprise.

As the four gunmen lay dead in the middle of the night, another voice told Harold Datson Jr. he wouldn't be able to hide behind a woman all his life. Also that if he wanted a fair fight to step in the moonlit night one on one. Holding Harold Datson Jr.'s arm, Mary Hagger told him it would not be one on one as more gunmen could be standing close by. He told her in a very low voice that she had risked her life many times for him, and it was his turn to do it for her. As he walked towards the gunman's voice, he assured him that he'd call his bluff, but that he knew he was not alone. Another silhouette appeared as the voice from the first gunman spoke saying that he'd be the one to draw fair and square with him.

Harold Datson Jr. stood for the first time head to head ready to draw against a man from his holster. The gunman also stood ready as he'd done so many times before, then laughed as he told him what he'd done to his father years ago. Trying to outwit the young man only made him focus more clearly as he drew his pistol out of his holster as fast as lightning. Sending two rounds of bullets into the gunman's chest. As he rolled on the ground, bullets from the second gunman sent dust in the air. Harold Datson Jr. once again shot into the dark night as the gunman fell to his knees and had no more bullets to shoot back. Standing up Harold Datson Jr. told him that he'd picked the wrong side to fight with as he unloaded the gun into the face of the gunman.

Not only was he fast, but he could also think of how to win a battle against more than one. The many lonely nights by himself had paid off. But the thoughts of his father lingered in his mind and would send him into another world of loneliness,for he wished each day that passed to see his father once more. Knowing that his father was still alive brought a great feeling to finally hope to see him again.

Keeping distance away from Oakwood was a must as he and Mary helped huddle everyone as close as they could as they moved on in the pitch dark night. After hours of walking, they came a- cross several big rocks which could be used to hide behind once the sun made its way over the empty land. The gunmen would once again come calling because if a man was known for the quickness of his guns, more needed to see if they could outdraw and even kill the other. He was a nobody, but once he'd killed hired Gunmen as he just had, he would become a target for anyone who wanted to make a name for himself. And if anyone knew the consequences, it would be his father who had once tamed outlaws as he'd also once used to be hired to catch and bring back outlaws dead or alive. The evil old man Earl Hessenger had ended any thoughts of ever using a gun again as he'd cut his trigger fingers off Harold Datson Sr. Now a man, his son held the magic in using a gun quicker than any man alive and the test for survival had just begun.

More smoke climbed up into the night's sky as another building was set on fire in Oakwood. Sitting in shock, Mary tried to hide her fear from the others. Then Harold Datson Jr. told her that when she first met him, she had told him it was OK to be afraid. And that it was OK to understand another day could mean it wouldn't be better off. And to sit out in the open night with her was better than sitting in the wine cellar all alone.

He put his arm around her shoulders as he promised to keep her safe because she had a Cowboy to deal with very soon. Smiling at each other, she laid her head on his shoulder and thanked him for understanding so much. He stared into the night sky's shining stars as he told Mary that she'd been the only mother he'd ever really known. She was proud of doing what she'd done for the young man as she'd taken good care of him. Now the respect was being shown as he had promised her safety to meet the Cowboy Bill Truette, who'd stolen her heart in moments when he'd held her in his strong arms promising to come back for her.

They all had risked their lives for one another, but no one was out of harm's way. Many had died in Oakwood when Hessenger had been there and now many were dying as the gunmen ran wild on the streets of the town.

One of the children stood next to Harold Datson Jr. and even though the night's darkness hid most things, the child handed him a holster with a good belt on it and told him it was better that the one with the rope around his waist. Shaking hands with the child, he asked where he'd gotten it and the child said it was from one of the dead gunmen who had fallen next to him earlier that night.

The rope that held the holster Harold Datson Jr. wore in the wine cellar now laid on the dirt to rot away. As he now wore a good holster with a belt that could hold the bullets he had in a box. Then another child came up to him handing him a hat from the same dead gunman, the first one had gotten the good holster from. In a way the children wanted him to know they appreciated the help he'd given them and knew that he would take care of them all. The three women stood in front of him with more food and water telling him how Mary had spoken very highly of him for many years. Harold Datson Jr. could now feel the responsibility on his shoulders.

CHAPTER 16

The flames from the fire from the Indian's camp were subsiding as the dawn's light began to shine over the mountains. For the day had finally come when death was to meet a soul so many had prayed for it to end. Hessenger in the hands of his most hated enemies now waited to be tortured, but the punishment he faced had no time limits. The longer it took for him to die, the more satisfied the Indian people would feel. Once it started, death would be the only way the torture would stop. Opening his eyes, Hessenger could only see Indian warriors standing around him as three walked up to him and began to whip him with water soaked switches from a tree. Beating his legs so he couldn't hold himself up.

The Cowboy then came into his vision, pulling at the handkerchief in his mouth very hard and fast. As he spoke to Hessenger he said, Welcome home, but not for long. Smiling, Truette told Hessenger, someone wanted to meet him. Yelling, Hessenger warned the cowboy of his men in Oakwood and that if he wanted to live to untie him as quick as he could. Bobby stood behind Hessenger with the hot P.G. branding iron. Shoving the hot branding iron onto Hessenger's back. The scream into the mountains echoed as Hessenger's body arched backward while still being tied to the trees from his limbs. After moments Hessenger dropped forward still tied to the trees, he could barely open his eyes as the young white Indian warrior passed by his side. The PG brand he'd burned on the young three year old child now brought memories back in Hessenger's mind. As they told him he should have killed the boy because the boy was going to kill him very slowly. With a spur from the evil old man's boots, the Cowboy stood holding it up against Hessenger's face. Then pressing the spur on the evil old man's face, Truette ripped the spur downward as fast as he could saying, You should have killed me, too. Blood gushed from the side of his face as his back was bleeding from the hot branding iron. Barely holding himself up, his legs were giving out from the beating with wet switches, but he tried to hang on as much as he could. Yelling once more, Hessenger promised everyone would die.

The old miner Harold Datson Sr. stood in front of him as the knife from the fire keeper was held in his hand red hot. Grabbing two fingers at a time, the old miner cut them away with a big smile on his face, as he told Hessenger that it would bring back memories as he showed him his own fingers of his hand. Before passing out, Hessenger's eyes had widened knowing who the old miner was.

Just a few moments had passed as cold river water was splashed onto Hessenger's face. Waking up in pain, the cowboy told him that the party had just started as the spur dug again on the other side of Hessenger's face. One by one the Indian warriors passed Hessenger's helpless body as each one threw Devil Head stickers still on the stems at his body. Then, as the circle came back around, the stems were pulled off in quick whacks. Sue Randalls Hessenger looked at Hessenger tied helpless to the trees as she walked over to him. She told him that she wished she could slap him. Looking back at Sue, the evil old man told her that he knew she still loved him and that it would be OK.

Sue stood for a moment and let Hessenger know that she could not slap him for fear of the blood running down his face Could get on her.

Walking to the fire keeper she motioned for a long limb that stuck out of the fire and burning on one end. Walking back to Hessenger's side, she laid the burning limb on the side of his neck. The mountains echoed once again as Hessenger yelled for mercy.

Out of nowhere Ring of Smoke, the baby wolf began to bite at the back of his right calf. Then on the left. Bobby, the white young Indian Warrior, now stood in front of Hessenger as he held a knife like the one that had been used to kill his mother after she was raped. He slowly began scalping one side of Hessenger's head. The echoes continued roaring into the mountains as Hessenger screamed in agony, begging for mercy. But no one really cared about him.

More cold river water awoke Hessenger as a mud puddle of blood and water laid under his feet. The young white Indian warrior Bobby returned to the evil old man's side with a piece of deer skin with the meat still attached which allowed the deer ticks to eat and stay in one place, until they were to be put into Hessenger's ears, They would eat until they reached the brain and drive the evil old man crazy or he would die first.

While the ticks made their way to the brain, the white Indian warrior made one inch cuts with the same knife all over Hessenger's body. Cutting down the weakened body, it was dragged out into the open land as the sun beamed down on an ant bed that had been stirred up, ready to attack anything in sight. Pouring honey on Hessenger's body, it laid to rest on the ant bed as they would leave nothing but his skeleton. Numb from pain in the ears and all over his wrecked body, Hessenger could no longer yell or even look out of his eyes, for thousands of red ants had taken control of his body forever.

***

Not having to worry about Hessenger anymore, the Cowboy Bill Truette, Sue, little Betsy, Bobby, the white Indian Warrior, and Ring of Smoke, the baby wolf, all went back to PG ranch. As the old miner Harold Datson Sr. rode his donkey behind them, more Indian warriors joined the band.

Inside PG ranch the Cowboy cleaned up and prepared a home cooked meal for everyone to eat and rest without having to worry about

Hessenger ever again. Night fell upon the PG ranch as the cowboy sat in his rocking chair outside smoking a cigarette looking towards the mountains, then towards where Oakwood would be. Truette could see the whiteness of what smoke would cause in the sky made him wonder about Mary Hagger and the people of Oakwood.

Hessenger had never returned and where his body now rested it for sure would never be found. Thinking back where he once worked, Truette took a big sigh and closed his eyes.

His boss was a big fellow with broad shoulders and a smile as big as his heart. He would always tell him that someday all this land with its outfit will belong to you, because you're the only son I really know.

In the moonlight, he could see many riders coming towards PG ranch. As he quickly got up and ran inside, he told everyone that the hired gunmen from Oakwood were on their way. They all had a rifle and could use it if they had to, but against the ruthless gunmen, they wouldn't have a chance. The old miner and a handful of Warriors lay out in the open ground all around the PG ranch and would fight till the end.

Closing the door behind him, the Cowboy stood on the porch waiting for the gunmen.

At the entrance of the corral, many horses lined up along the fence in twos and threes. To the back of them rolled a chuck wagon.

The voice that broke the thick silence in the dark night asked for Truette the Cowboy. Then the cowboy spoke back saying that he was Bill Truette and to state their business. The first voice replied that he was with the Silver Star ranch and had come to help. In the pitch dark night, the Cowboy Bill Truette took off his hat and threw it in the air running inside the PG ranch bending over to pick up little Betsy. Heading back out the door he told everyone his help had arrived as he went to the corral to meet the ranch hands from the Double S ranch, The Silver Star.

As the Silver Star's men began to camp out for the night around PG ranch, the boss of the outfit was helped off the wagon, but he could speak in a very low pained voice. Truette's boss had been sick for a while as the cancer ate away into the heart. Inside the PG ranch the old boss from the Silver Star spoke to the Cowboy that he would not last much longer and had been waiting to hear from him for many years.

The old miner sat quietly in the room looking at the Silver Star's boss's eyes. Then as their eyes focused on each other, the boss of the Silver Star ranch asked if they'd ever met. Not wanting anyone to know who he used to be, he shook his head no as he dropped his eyes to the floor. The Silver Star boss looked at the branding iron$_7$ spurs and holster with a gun it for a while.

He told the old miner again, Your eyes tell me a story with a name I once knew of a man who once wore those spurs and gun with those letters on them HD. Nodding his head the Silver Star boss looked at the old miner and said, Eyes never lie and they tell me you're the famous gunslinger Harold Datson Sr.

Truette stood up from his chair and spoke to the old miner letting him know that it had not been right not to claim the branding iron, spurs and gun when it rightly belonged to him. Harold Datson Sr. dropped his head in shame as he began telling the Silver Star boss and Bill Truette what had happened to him.

As he spoke of the day Hessenger had come calling on him to work as a hired gunman.

Tears rolled down his face as he spoke of the night his son was taken away into Oakwood. As he took off his gloves and showed them his hands, saying how he'd lost his fingers for not wanting to work for Hessenger.

As the Silver Star boss heard the name Earl Hessenger, he tried to get up, falling to the floor and coughing as he said, "I need to find that man as quick as I can." He spoke of how he knew the evil old man and his wicked ways, but could never catch him when he was a captain for the army.

Smiling, the Cowboy Bill Truette told the Silver Star boss that Earl Hessenger had been put to death earlier that day and not to worry about him anymore. Then the Cowboy slowly turned around looking into the fireplace that lit the room in a gentle glow. In the midst of that peaceful moment, the Silver Star boss told the Cowboy that all the years of knowing him he could tell when something bothered him because he knew him like a son. One hundred ruthless gunmen in Oakwood needed to be stopped, the Cowboy told his old friend and that's why he'd sent him the message.

The Silver Star boss told the Cowboy that the boy who had brought the message had returned with them and camped outside with the others but hardly ever spoke. Truette turned around looking at his boss and said that he wanted to speak with the boy who'd brought the message. In moments the boy, a red head, with freckles, skinny, tall, blue eyes and curly hair, stood in front of Bill Truette. As the cowboy spoke to the boy about the message he told the boy that the lady at the general store Mary Hagger had sent the message and if the boy knew her. He dropped his head as the Silver Star boss told Bill Truette that the boy hardly spoke to anyone.

Truette took three steps as he stood in front of the boy asking him if he was worried about Oakwood. The boy said not really, only one person. Truette asked if it had been Mary and the boy said yes. As he walked over to the fireplace, staring at the flames, he said he was worried about her because she was his mother.

Truette knew in his heart that Mary had liked him or she would have never sent her own son. He told the boy that he was the one they call the Cowboy. The boy's eyes looked at Bill Truette and he knew his mother had told her son about him.

The Cowboy told the boy his mother was and would be OK and in the morning everyone would ride into Oakwood and clean the town out of gunmen.

The night seemed to take forever as Truette's thoughts took him in to another world of past events in his life. Mary at the top of his mind would not go away. She had risked her life many times in Oakwood and had risked the life of her own son. As she had sent him with the message for help to the Double S ranch. Now half of the Silver Star ranch lay out on the grounds of the PG ranch ready to help save Oakwood. Truette's boss wasn't looking too good as the cancer ate away around his heart. But he had kept his word that if the cowboy ever sent for help, he would come himself. Bringing half his men was even more than any man could ask for out in the open wild land.

The Silver Star ranch was a big family type of ranch as no outlaws ever got hired. Only a man who'd worked for the law or had real family members tied to marshals, deputy sheriffs, scouts, as Truette once used to be, could hire on as hands for the Double S ranch.

Every man that lay out on the grounds of the PG ranch was a trained killer, but only for the right reasons. And Oakwood was the right reason any man with a good heart should help bring down the gunmen that waited.

As the night's moon slowly made its way over the mountains, the dawn's light began to show on the other side of the horizon.

It was time to move on as the men from the Silver Star ranch had rested only one night. The weakened Double S ranch boss would not go on as he'd told the cowboy, Bill Truette to go on without him because he would only slow them down. Riding all day, the cowboy out in front like old times, but this time no clues on the ground had to be looked for as Oakwood was the place to go where the fight against the ruthless gunmen would take place. No one was promised to return and none of the gunmen were promised to let live. It would be a fight till only one side stood up alive.

As Bill Truette motioned a spot to rest for the night, campfires lit up along the open land as the men from the Double S ranch had laid their lives of the line for the cowboy who was like a family member to them. The night crawled by slowly for everyone but they all needed a rest as well as the horses.

Riding out once more, Bill Truette told the riders to pass the word down the line that Oakwood would come into view late that day and a few hours would be given to rest as he planned to attack at night. To outwit the gunmen in Oakwood was a must because he knew his help would give them a better chance to live.

CHAPTER 17

Three nights had passed since Mary Hagger and Harold Datson Jr. had escaped from Oakwood. But still in the embrace of gunmen who camped nearby, ready to attack at anytime. All the children kept the gunmen at bay, but food and water had run out the day before, the rifles were empty and the gunmen wanted to end everyone's lives for good.

Having to stay in the same place for three nights was not what Mary Hagger had planned, but moving any further would surely cause the death of all. The gunmen had pinned them down as now and then played with bullets,as the gunmen shot very close to them. What they really wanted was for Mary Hagger or Harold Datson Jr. and any of the women and children to try to make a run for it so they could shoot them in cold blood. At the same time, Truette and about twenty ranch hands from the Silver Star ranch were crawling quietly into Oakwood. The plan was to scatter out into the darkened town while the rest of the ranch hands surrounded Oakwood and opened fire to any gunmen who tried to leave. Next to Truette's side was the Indian messenger who'd gone into Oakwood and made it out safe as he'd killed six one night and seven the next night. Now all twenty Silver Star ranch hands along with Truette and the Indian messenger crawled as they cut the throats of gunmen or stabbed them in their hearts. Each Silver Star ranch hand knew how to take a life and not get caught.

Gunmen laid dead all throughout Oakwood with their throats cut or their heart stabbed from the front of the chest or through their backs. In some areas of the town, gunmen hanged from their necks from buildings or out of the windows of their rooms. Some were killed as they slept. But none ever saw death coming only when death was right on them as their lives were taken away.

The eerie silence was broken as the shooting began. It had been a few gunmen on the top edges of the hotel who'd seen some Silver Star ranch hands crawling toward the general store along with Truette and the Indian messenger. Kicking in the doors and running inside, They were safe for a moment until the general store was set on fire. The bright flames had been seen from the other Silver Star ranch hands that surrounded Oakwood. It was time to move in and kill anything standing as the plan was said to be. Only the ruthless gunmen stood because of pride and not knowing the plan itself.

As the gunfire lit up the town, many gunmen could tell that the end was at hand. As some would yell out in the darkened night to please not shoot because they were coming out. When the plan to bring down the hired gunmen was put out it meant that not one gunman would be left to live and tell about it, or live to begin what Hessenger had started twelve years ago, or longer.

As the dawn's light began to appear, Oakwood stood still with smoke from the previous night's fires. More gunmen hid inside some of the buildings as they yelled out the windows that they would surrender. But none could be trusted even though they threw out their guns first and walked into the streets of Oakwood. They were shot down any ways because all the Silver Star ranch hands had no room in their saddles to take them to jail. In fact, there was no jail in Oakwood since the day Earl Hessenger had taken over twelve years before.

As the Sliver Star ranch hands walked through the town of Oakwood, the people slowly opened up doors as they looked on.

Many dead gunmen laid in the streets of Oakwood as the Silver Star ranch hands had no intentions of picking them up. The Cowboy Bill Truette and the Indian messenger stood next to where the burnt down general store used to be. Looking at the ground for clues, the saw two sets of footprints walk from the side of the place the general store used to be. Then stop to turn around and walk then walk again. Yards before the footprints had stopped and turned around laid two dead gunmen with bullet holes in them in the exact same spot. Whoever it had been had shot and killed the two gunmen then continued to walk out of town along with about a dozen or more with them. Someone was running away and the Cowboy hoped it was Mary Hagger.

Riding his horse Truette and many more Silver Star ranch hands followed their trusted friend. If anyone knew how to follow a trail, it would be Truette for it had been his job as a scout many years ago. To follow and stay with a trail was what he was good at. Hours later his instincts had paid off for he could hear gunplay echo in the air. Sending more shots of his own was to let whoever it was up ahead that someone else was on the way. As the gunmen heard and later saw the Silver Star Ranch hands approaching, they took off in all directions to try to get away. But it was too late as the Silver Star ranch hands followed just as fast. Truette rode into the direction of some rocks as he called out that he was there to help. Mary ran out first as the Cowboy saw her and jumped off his horse to meet her. She ran as fast as she could to him. With open arms each met as they hugged each other tight. The Cowboy told her he had promised to come back for her.

Harold Datson Jr. walked out from the rocks as he met Truette for the first time. He said that Mary spoke highly of him and it was an honor to meet him. The Cowboy looked at the young man and asked if his name could be Harold Datson Jr. The young man looked at Mary then back at the Cowboy as he said the one and only. Shaking his hand saying Your Dad spoke of a young man like you and he's waiting at the PG ranch for you safe and sound.

A big smile over took Harold Datson Jr.'s emotions. He stood looking at Mary as tears rolled down his face. He told her it was because of her he'd survived twelve years in the wine cellar and that if she hadn't helped he'd surely be dead right now. Then out of nowhere, a gunman stood looking at the Cowboy as he spoke of not running like the rest. Harold Datson Jr. walked in between the cowboy and the gunman. As he told the gunman, his voice sounded familiar to the Cowboy, a lot like the voice of the coward who barged in the hotel asking Hessenger if he could go potty. The rage over swept the gunman who forgot all about Truette as he went for his guns. A bullet hit him in between the eyes and never had a chance to draw his guns, but only grabbed the butts. Harold Datson Jr. was the fastest draw Truette had ever seen and as the young man turned around, he told the cowboy that Mary had taught him every trick he knew as he smiled at her. Truette looked at Mary as he joked by asking if she would show him that trick. All three laughed as they walked up to the rocks, then the children stood up along with the three women.

Heading back into Oakwood, everyone was happy as the children found their parents. They walked away, but not before thanking Mary Hagger, Harold Datson Jr., Bill Truette and the brave Silver Star ranch hands who had come to help.

Everything Mary Hagger had worked for lay before her eyes burnt. But next to her she had a man who she could feel would keep her safe. As he spoke about a ranch in the meadows called the PG ranch.

The town began to go up again as the Silver Star ranch hands followed Truette's wagon out of town. Arriving at the PG ranch, Ring of Smoke stood on the porch as he howled in the late evening. Next to the Little Wolf, the white Indian warrior Bobby was holding little Betsy in his arms. Sue walked out onto the porch as she smiled at her Uncle Bill. Slowly the old miner made his way out the door. As the two Harold Datson's eyes met, they each knew in an instant that they were and ran to hug each other.

Harold Datson Sr. was now reunited with his son Harold Datson Jr. who cried together as everyone else entered the door of the PG ranch. Looking into the eyes of Truette, Sue knew he was looking back. As he slowly turned around, the look on Sue's face told the story. The Silver Star ranch boss had died the night before as the cancer had taken its toll. Walking up to the Cowboy Sue hugged him as she said that he told her to tell him he loved him more than a son and that he'd left the Cowboy all the deeds to the Silver Star ranch.

Walking back out the door of the PG ranch, the Cowboy looked at the men from the Silver Star ranch. No words were needed as all of them stood to the side of the PG ranch, where the graves of Truette's sister and brother-in-law and his wife and children laid to rest. Sue and Bobby the white Indian warrior had buried the Silver Star boss. Walking over to the graves, "The Cowboy", Bill Truette fell to his knees as he began to pray. After a while the Silver Star ranch hands began making camp fires for the night for the morning's sun would start their long journey home.

Inside the PG ranch, the glow from the chimney's fire gave light to reveal the glistening tears still on the Cowboy's face.

For his boss was laid to rest and had only lived long enough to see and help Truette once more like old times.

The night seemed to take forever as the Cowboy walked out the door. Looking at all the men from the Silver Star ranch, Truette spoke to them and thanked them all. He asked how many men had been lost as the foreman for the Silver Star ranch spoke; he hung his head to the ground as he held his hat to his chest and said, only one, meaning the boss.

Taking a few steps off the porch, the Cowboy handed the deeds to the Silver Star ranch's foreman. As he told him that the PG ranch was his home and he could not leave his family behind or take them away. He knew the deeds rightly belonged to the foreman as he'd taken good care of the Silver Star ranch boss for years.

The trail of men leaving the PG ranch were the bravest men Truette had ever known. He wished he could go along once more like old times. Then Ring of Smoke brought him back from an endless stare at the line of men leaving the PG ranch. Getting down on one knee to pick up his little wolf, the Cowboy looked up into the smaller mountains. To the side of the ranch a silhouette along the top stood a long line of Indian warriors ready to honor him back home.

As the door opened, Harold Datson Jr. and his father stood looking at Truette. The years the Cowboy had lived not only brought him great wisdom as he could read the old miner's mind.

He shook his head and said it belongs to you anyway. The Cowboy knew that Harold Datson Sr. wanted to give the old gun on the wall he'd used in his younger days to his son. As he made his way back inside he whispered to both of them that Oakwood was going to need a good sheriff anyway. Then he smiled and walked passed them.

CHAPTER 18

In the Indian camp the native people danced to the sounds of drums. As the powwow fire grew higher and higher. But in the face of the aged Indian Chief, you could tell his heart was not full. Something was missing as he sat staring at the dancers.

Then a howl of a wolf came closer and closer as the Chief stood tall over the fire he could see riders on horseback along with a wagon approaching. Seeing little Betsy sitting on the donkey brought a big smile to his face, but his eyes searched beyond everything in sight.

As the wagon came to a stop, Bobby the white Indian warrior who had been raised by the Indian Chief were now looking at each other. As the Cowboy jumped off the wagon, he helped Sue and the old miner to the ground from the back of the wagon; Mary was helped off as well. As Truette led the way to the powwow, Bobby took hold of the donkey and led it into the midst of the Indian camp. Harold Datson Jr. and the red head kid, Mary Hagger's son, dismounted their horses as they looked on at the dancers.

Harold Datson Sr. and the Indian Chief gave each other big hugs as Harold Datson Jr. was motioned to come over to meet the Indian Chief. Hugging Bobby again, the Indian Chief could not hold back the tears of his sparkling eyes. But they were tears of joy from reuniting with loved ones.

Mary stood still as the dancers moved all around her. Then the fire keeper walked up to her. Looking into her eyes, he spoke in his native tongue while the old miner Harold Datson Sr. translated that a child would come forth soon to mend the cowboy's heart. And to make her happy again. Truette was the Cowboy Harold Datson, Sr. spoke of as he put his arm around Mary's son's shoulders. You could see the scar on the cowboy's face in the light of the fire from Hessenger's spurs. Dancing toward the Cowboy, the Indian dancers picked up the cowboy, as others joined in to hold the cowboy in the air. As they danced around the fire, the drums beat through the night. Truette had become a hero to the Indian people as well as to the people of Oakwood.

Harold Datson Jr. and Sue Randalls Hessenger watched the dancers standing next to each other without knowing it. At the same time, they spoke the same words, Where's Betsy? Then a smile followed their words as little Betsy ran to them and stood in between them while holding one hand of each. The look in their eyes was one of love meant to be as they both had a gift no treasure could ever buy and it was little Betsy herself. Harold Datson Sr. wiped away the tears from his eyes as he sat next to his friend the Indian Chief when he saw his son with Sue and Betsy.

The night had been long as the morning sun began to shine. Truette and Mary got on the wagon as Harold Datson Jr. helped Sue and little Betsy. Mounting his horses, he waited for Mary's son to mount his. The old miner Harold Datson Sr. got on his donkey. As the Indian Chief looked on, the white warrior jumped on the back of his horse. Waving good-bye to the native people, they all rode away. Tears rolled down the Indian Chief's face as his only son the white Indian warrior Bobby rode away.

Miles away into the open land the Cowboy kept looking at the Indian warrior Bobby his nephew. The look spoke for itself as a part of Bobby had been left behind. Stopping the wagon Truette got off and walked over to Harold Datson Sr. who was on his donkey. As they spoke looking back toward the Indian camp, everyone wondered what was going on. The old miner spoke in a native tongue to Bobby the white Indian warrior as his eyes lit up, then turned his horse and took off and stopped for a moment as in the distance you could see he waved good-bye. The Cowboy got back on the wagon and said that Bobby was best off with the Indian Chief and he knew Bobby would come around often anyways. Standing in the searing sun in the sky, the Indian Chief looked on. An eagle flew over, then in a huge circle it flew over once more. The dust in the distance caught the Indian Chief's eye as he kept looking, the smile on his face got bigger and bigger. As Bobby rode closer, all the Indian warriors echoed through the mountains as they yelled at their brother back to the camp in happiness. Yards away from the camp, Bobby jumped off his horse turning to the only father he really knew, the Indian chief himself.

As the wagon rolled on towards the PG Ranch, the Cowboy began wondering about Hessenger's will. Then he looked at Sue and little Betsy. One of them would be the keeper of all his treasures. But Oakwood would no longer belong to anyone.

Life at the PG ranch returned to normal. Mary gave birth to a son who was named Bill Truette Jr.

Sue and Harold Datson Jr. moved to town where they got married and he became the new sheriff. Mary's red headed son Dusty became the deputy.

Oakwood began to grow as young guns once in a while who wanted a name for themselves would come calling on Harold Datson Jr. But his lightning fast draws were too much as word got out he'd earned the respect from both sides of the law. Taming the land was one thing, staying alive had been another for Harold Datson Jr. But the rewards of having someone like Mary helped him when he'd been a prisoner in the wine cellar had paid off tremendously.

And each time Harold Datson Jr. had to kill, it would be for the right reasons.

***

Ring of Smoke

As time went on, the old Indian Chief had died as Bobby the White Indian warrior had become the new Chief. Each morning silhouettes of Indian outlined the mountain tops. As the new Chief Bobby watched the PG ranch, tears would roll down his face as he looked towards the graves.

Devil's Dm Desert remained the same as Crystal Pit Canyons' deadly animals roamed through the nights, the circle of life for survival continued on.

Harold Datson Sr. moved to the PG ranch as the young Bill Truette Jr. grew, the old miner would show the young boy his talents with his guns. Another gunman was in the making as he was taught to be a scout as well.

Ring of Smoke grew to become a huge wolf as he'd taken off with a pack of wolves. Through the nights, his howls could be heard and it seemed Ring of Smoke would always be watching the PG ranch.

The Cowboy had pinned the little rag doll above the fireplace where the branding iron and spurs of HD still hung. For Harold Datson Jr. proudly wore the gun his father once did, but he was even faster as he'd learned on his own. A dream come true, Oakwood had become a peaceful town. As Dusty would watch the ranch, Sue, little Betsy and Harold Datson, Jr. would visit the PG ranch once in a while.

Truette would always sit outside the porch sipping on a cup of coffee.

As he'd rock back and forth on his rocking chair the thoughts that ran through his head brought tears to the edges of his eyes, but he was blessed with his new family and Indian friends as they would watch him from the mountain tops.

After a good cup of coffee each morning in the rocking chair, the cowboy would pray at the graves next to the PG ranch. When Sue was visiting she would wake up early each day looking for her uncle. One morning she found the rocking chair moving with the wind and she started looking around as crazy thoughts lingered in her mind. Searching for the Cowboy, she'd come across him at the graves. As she watched him spending moments on each grave, she was puzzled why he'd stop to pray on the PG grave. As she stepped closer trying to hear him speak, she stepped on a twig which made him spin around with his gun in his hand. Slowly putting it back in his holster he told her to please not ever sneak up on him again. She wondered why he'd been praying on the PG grave and asked why. He smiled at Sue walking past her saying It's not a person and it's not an animal and if she really wanted to know, he told her there's a shovel as he winked at her and went inside the PG ranch. Finally, he had a place he called his home. Standing on the porch, Sue looked into the snow capped mountains then down below as the beautiful meadows held silhouettes of hundreds of riders on horseback approaching. Stepping back out of the door of the PG ranch, Truette stood next to Sue as he put his arm around her. He noticed that she was frozen in shock. Then seeing the images of men on horseback, he told her it's about time they showed up and told her he'd sent for more cattle from the Silver Star ranch. Sue closed her eyes and asked the Cowboy if he could hear Ring of Smoke in the distance. As she opened her eyes, she saw the wolf standing on the PG grave.

THE END

Felix Flores, Jr.

About the Author

Felix Flores Jr. was born in Lubbock, Texas. From an early age, Westerns have always been his favorite movies and books.

Now single and in his 50's, it's time to tell the world the Western stories in his mind.

Having lived a life of crime, his craving to write Westerns grew even more as he's sat alone for many years in prison cells. He spends his time working prison duties and writing each day.

He has been in prison for over 20 years and will soon be free. Upon his release, he plans on opening a wood shop and writing more Westerns. He has currently finished both *Circle of Death* and *Circle of Death The Promises* both soon to be published by Midnight Express Books.

Felix Flores, Jr.

www.ingramcontent.com/pod-product-compliance
Lightning Source LLC
Chambersburg PA
CBHW071252130626
46556CB00003B/1287